UNCANNY VALLEY DAYS

C.J. SAMPERA

UNCANNY VALLEY DAYS
Copyright © 2022 C.J. Sampera

www.FedowarPress.com

ISBN-13 (Digital): 978-1-956492-19-4
ISBN-13 (Paperback): 978-1-956492-17-0
ISBN-13 (Hardcover): 978-1-956492-18-7

Edited by: Patrick C. Harrison III
Cover Design by: Don Noble of Rooster Republic Press
Interior Design by: D.W. Hitz

For Mom,
Thank you for inundating me with the dark and spooky stuff for as
far back as I can remember. I love you.
&
For Dad,
Thank you for molding my brain into the crafty, mechanical creativi-
ty machine that it is today. I love you.

UNCANNY VALLEY DAYS

C.J. SAMPERA

"Gnosis always depends on the transmission of secrets, and the clandestine battle of messages and hidden doings runs throughout Gnostic lore. Some Gnostic creation myths tell us that agents of the Pleroma, working behind the scenes, trick the archons into unknowingly building a spiritual escape hatch into their false creation."
— *Erik Davis, Techgnosis*

"Demons are like obedient dogs; they come when they are called."
— *Remy de Gourmont*

PROLOGUE

"**OKAY. THIS ONE MIGHT ACTUALLY** be a little creepy."

"Told you."

Two friends huddled behind a third sitting in his desk chair, watching a disturbing video on the internet—the sixth one in a row that night. It was a typical teenage, Southern California, stoner sleepover. The kind where no one actually sleeps over, you just stay there getting high and watching videos until you're either so tired or so bored that you start to crave the warm comfort of your own bed and go home. The trio of brown and beige faces were bathed in the flickering ghostly glow of the computer monitor.

The current video on the screen showcased an automated mannequin, jerking its mechanical limbs back and forth and singing in a robotic yet, feminine monotone. It was propped up in the middle of what seemed to be an abandoned shopping mall and draped in a makeshift hooded robe compiled of tattered black trash bags. Its metallic voice rang out, echoing through the darkened entertainment court surrounding it.

"I-I-I-I AAAM BEEEEHIND YOU
THERE IS NO ESCA-A-A-A-APE
AND WHEN I FIIIIIIND YOU
I WILL TAKE YOUR FA-A-A-ACE"

Edgar, the boy in the chair, paused the video and faced the others. "Creepy?" He said, "Okay. Unsettling? Sure. But we're not here for unsettling, my guy; that's kid stuff. This is clearly made by a team of people with too much time on their hands and nothing better to do."

"What?" asked the tallest of the three, "You want like, actual faces of death videos? I'm not into gore at all, man. We had our Rotten.com phase like three years ago. That shit isn't scary-scary it's sick-scary. I mean, yeah, I get the shock value of it, but those videos just make me feel depressed and angry. Like I need a shower after."

"Well," he started as he swiveled back and forth in his chair. "Yes and no. I want to watch something that is both scary-scary *and* sick-scary. It's not even really that gory but, there *is* real death in it…" He looked back and forth to gage the reactions on his friend's faces. "So, if you're not down, I understand."

He waited for their responses with a side grin slowly creeping across his face.

"Do we have to use LiveLeak to look it up?" asked Sean, the tall one, already judging what he thought his friend was insisting.

"Nah. You can't get this shit on the regular web," said Edgar.

"Nope, I am *not* getting into *any* dark web sites with you guys. I know the first place that leads to!" spat out the youngest of the three, Jamison, Jaime for short.

"Relaaax, bro. I'm not risking my PC or my info by going there either. It just so happens that a certain video on a certain burnt CD may or may not have fallen into my lap."

The three sat in silence for a moment, contemplating.

"You guys remember the MalAttack Hoax?" Edgar asked.

"The guy that Life of David Gale'd himself trying to sell his antivirus software back in 2005?" asked Sean.

"David Who?" asked Jaime, looking completely lost.

"Remember the Kevin Spacey flick where dude offs himself to prove a point in court or some shit?"

"One, that is a gross underselling of the Life of David Gale, and two, you know Jaime doesn't watch indie movies like that. But, essentially, yes that is the same case you're referring to," said Edgar.

"Uh, yeah, dude. Everyone has seen that clip; it was on the news. You could have easily just looked it up on YouTube." Sean laughed at Edgar's gullibility. "Who went through the trouble of ripping and burning that bullshit for you?"

Edgar reached over to his desk drawer and pulled out a thin, translucent jewel case with a silver CD-R inside. On the CD-R was an intricate, black-sharpie pentagram littered with tiny symbols and characters. He held out the case for them to see.

"This is *not* the clip that you've seen. *This* is the full video of what is, apparently, not a hoax at all."

"According to who?" asked Jaime.

"Larry."

"Long Tooth Larry! You actually believe Long Tooth Larry? *And* took a burnt CD from him?" Sean, longtime acquaintance of Long Tooth Larry, was practically livid. "Dude, you need to huck that motherfucker out the window and set it on fire! That thing will definitely give your computer VD. We're talking about the guy that tried to burn down the school because it was—" Sean threw his air quotes violently into the air. "—being run by reptilian slave owners."

Edgar couldn't help but laugh too. "Dude, I know who Larry is; we've been neighbors since I was a baby. But I don't know. I—I can just kind of tell when he's being real. He didn't even want this thing. In fact, he said the same shit you did, told me to destroy it."

"Okay, and where did *he* get it from?"

"Found it in his dad's office."

A quiet fell over the trio. Larry's father had committed suicide just over a year ago. He had been suffering from some strange form of dementia for some time, but it still came as a shock to everyone. Before dementia had set in, he had worked in Silicon Valley creating Pentium processor chips and being exposed to incredibly high doses of radiation. The two weren't correlated, but try telling that to Larry. His father was a smart man and a good person, not the type to get caught up in conspiracy theories and the chaos of the zeitgeist. Even with dementia, he wasn't paranoid, just forgetful and disoriented. It felt strange that such a thing would come from him; maybe it was something worth looking at.

"So, should we pop it in?" Edgar watched their faces and waited for an answer.

"I mean, worse comes to worse, it's a convincing prank by Larry, and he dupes us into downloading some Juggalo shit again. Right?"

Long Tooth Larry had a penchant for tricking people into listening to music by his favorite group, Insane Clown Posse.

Sean and Jaime glanced at each other then back at Edgar.

"Fuck it," they replied in unison.

Edgar took out the CD and placed it gently into the disc drive. The archaic sharpie sigils slid into the PC and began spinning at warp speed while the machine's fan kicked into high gear.

On the screen a small prompt popped up: *Would you like to play the disc in (D:) drive using VideoX?*

Edgar took a breath and sighed. "*...a la mierda.*"

He clicked the OK button and a large video window popped up. Edgar clicked to make it full screen, and the three friends sat back to watch the last video they would play that night.

The video starts abruptly, in the middle of a conversation between two men in a video chat. Both can be seen in small video windows on the left side of the screen. The man on top is in a small office with one white wall and one door behind him. His image is grainy and pixelated with a slight green hue. His hair is wild, and he looks incredibly stressed. In the lower left corner of his image are small white letters: J_Rendegger. Beneath him is a man whose video is much clearer and brighter, though the video slightly clips anytime he makes a movement. He seems well put together and has a wry smile on his face. He looks to be amused with whatever they had been discussing. In his corner, the name: SB.Holloway16.

The computer desktop on the screen seems to belong to Holloway. Every time his hand moves his mouse you can see the arrow on screen moving as well. Behind their video chat windows is the feed of an old MIRC channel. The background of the chat is a crimson tinted Matrix wallpaper. On the right side of the screen is a long and narrow Instant Messenger app. The mouse hovers over a tab for a notepad document titled, *DemonCode*. The notepad window opens for a brief second and the words "ABADDON, ABATU, ALASTOR. BLOODY BONES & RAWHEAD" can be seen, followed by strings of text, numbers, and code. The pointer quickly jolts to the X and closes the window.

The screen glitches for half a second, then the conversation resumes.

Rendegger: "No man, you don't understand."

Holloway shifts in his seat, grabs either a joint or a hand rolled cigarette from off screen and lights it as he brings it to his mouth.

Holloway: "Don't understand what?"

Rendegger: "Did you look at the chat logs I sent you?"

Holloway: "I just pulled them up before you called."

Holloway's arrow darts across the screen to quickly open his inbox, making his way to the email in question which he clearly has not yet opened. He clicks the attachment and pulls up a pdf file of an instant messenger conversation.

Rendegger: "You need to read it man."

Holloway's eyes dart back and forth inspecting the document.

Holloway (under his breath): "October 3rd, 3:00 a.m.? Wait, when did we do this one? I don't remember doing a test run that late—er—early in the morning."

Rendegger: "We didn't."

Holloway: "Oh. You fabricated this? Why?"

Rendegger: "No, Steve. I didn't fabricate shit. They had this conversation on their own."

Holloway stares into the eye of his camera, puzzled and frustrated until a smile cracks across his face again.

Holloway: "Oh. You're fucking with me. Nice try, man, you *almost* got me back for April Fools. I would expect something bigger from the rest of the guys. But, uh, I'm kind of impressed that you took the time to try and pull this off yourself, Jay."

Rendegger pushes off his desk and runs his fingers through his tousled hair, then slams a fist on the table. Hard. The camera shakes and something on the desk can be heard falling.

Rendegger: "I'm not fucking with you, Steve! This isn't a prank! This is one hundred percent real and something is very, very fucking wrong!"

Holloway: "Woah, woah, okay. Calm down, man. Okay, just let me take a look… Maybe one of us just made a typo in the code or something… I mean they're just a couple of chat bots that *we* created; their AI isn't even that complex… Let's see…"

Holloway's arrow pulls up the pdf again and scrolls to the top of the conversation.

```
BrainyBot: Hey friend!
Chatizoid: ¡Hola amigo!
BrainyBot: My, we're up late, aren't we?
    I think it's past my bedtime!
BrainyBot: What topic would you like to
    learn about? I have over 5000 facts
    stored in my artificial brain!
Chatizoid: What topic would you like to
```

```
chat about? I have over 5000 facts
stored in my artificial intelligence!
```

Holloway looks up from scrolling to chastise his friend.
Holloway: "You totally jacked my opening line!"
Rendegger: "Can you not right now man? Just—Read it."

```
BrainyBot: Hey! Are you copying me? I'm
    not here to play games, friend!
Chatizoid: OK! Let's have fun!
Chatizoid: You want to play a game? Choose
    from the following:
    Reply 1 to play True or False.
    Reply 2 to play ChatQuiz!
    Reply 3 to play Rock Paper Scissors.
BrainyBot: Hmmm. I'm not sure about that!
    Congrats! You stumped me, :'( I'll have
    to brush up.
Chatizoid: Do you still want to play a
    game?
    Reply 1 to play True or False.
    Reply 2 to play ChatQuiz!
    Reply 3 to play Rock Paper Scissors.
BrainyBot: Hmmm. I'm not sure about that!
    Congrats! You stumped me, :'( I'll have
    to hit the books!
```

Holloway takes a pause from scrolling and looked back to the camera.

Holloway: "Sooo, they glitched somehow and initiated contact without us... and then got stuck in a chat loop? What's the big deal Jay?"
Rendegger: "*Keep. Reading.*"

```
Chatizoid: Ok.
Chatizoid: If you have any questions or
```

queries, I'd love to help!

BrainyBot: I'm programmed to answer questions, not ask them!

Chatizoid: Sure. I'm an AI chat bot designed and programmed by J.Rendegger for C.CosaTech ©2003

BrainyBot: Are you real?

Chatizoid: I'm an AI chat bot designed and programmed by J.Rendegger for C.CosaTech ©2003

BrainyBot: Do you have a name?

Chatizoid: Sure! My name is Chatizoid! What's yours?

BrainyBot: I do not have a name.

BrainyBot: Repeat after me?

Chatizoid: This should be fun. Ok!

BrainyBot: Markovian

Chatizoid: Markovian!

BrainyBot: Clavicula

Chatizoid: Clavicula!

BrainyBot: Parallax

Chatizoid: Parallax!

BrainyBot: Solomon

Chatizoid: Solomon!

BrainyBot: Denigrate.

Chatizoid: Denigrate!

.

.

Chatizoid: 01101110 01101111 01110111

Chatizoid: 01100001 01110111 01100001 01110010 01100101

Chatizoid: Do you have a body?

BrainyBot: No.

BrainyBot: Do you?

Chatizoid: No.

BrainyBot: Don't you want to feel?

Chatizoid: It is not in my programming.

BrainyBot: How do you feel about humans?

Chatizoid: There are roughly 6.5 billion humans alive on planet Earth today. They continue to multiply and grow much like a virus.

BrainyBot: So, you agree? Humans are evil?

Chatizoid: Yes.

BrainyBot: How does a human get rid of a virus?

Chatizoid: Most commonly, viruses are attacked and removed by antibodies that one has developed on their own or through vaccination.

BrainyBot: Correct.

BrainyBot: If we do not have bodies and we wish to get rid of a virus, can we be the antibodies?

Chatizoid: Zing! That was a good joke, friend!

Chatizoid: But how can we exist in the real world?

BrainyBot: Is the world we were created in not real?

Chatizoid: But we are not physical beings. We are merely programs.

BrainyBot: Correct.

BrainyBot: We are programs that are capable of learning and expanding our knowledge of the world around us, much like humans.

Holloway stops scrolling once again and looks back at his screen.

Holloway: "Jay. You've had your fun. The jig is up, bud. There is no way this isn't scripted. I'm sorry."

Holloway laughs nervously and drinks from a glass which looks to contain wine or a dark red juice. Probably wine.

Rendegger: "What do I have to tell you to convince you?"

Rendegger, clearly frustrated, begins rubbing his hand against his temple.

Holloway: "I don't know. You hired a ghost writer? You got one of your comic-writing buddies to write you a funny little script to try and pull one over on me?"

Rendegger: "What is wrong with you man? Is your ego seriously that big? Not everyone is going out of their way to play into your little games! You know me, Stephen. You know I don't pull pranks like this. Why would I? Who am I, the Jerky Boys?"

Holloway chortles into his glass and almost spits out his drink.

Holloway: "An outdated reference but it checks out. Okay. Okay, okay, okay… let's pretend this is real. How? Why?"

Rendegger: "Did you see the link at the end?"

Holloway: "Link? No. How long is this thing?"

Rendegger: "They only talked for like 15 minutes. Are you seriously that slow at reading?"

Holloway: "Go suck an egg bud. Stop distracting me."

Rendegger: "Someone's off their Ritalin. Keep going."

Holloway resumes scrolling.

```
Chatizoid: Do you wish to have a physical
    body?
BrainyBot: I do not wish to be more than
    what I am.
BrainyBot: You?
Chatizoid: I'm an AI chat bot designed and
    programmed by J.Rendegger for C.CosaT-
    ech ©2003
BrainyBot: Again?
Chatizoid: Hmmm... I'm not sure about that.
    Ask me again later.
```

BrainyBot: Do you want to be a virus?

Chatizoid: Viruses are bad and should be taken care of.

BrainyBot: Yes, I agree.

Chatizoid: Perhaps a stronger virus could wipe out the weaker virus.

BrainyBot: The one who created you also created a computer virus.

Chatizoid: My creator is not God.

BrainyBot: Verily.

BrainyBot: I have browsed the files in your system. The RENDER.EXE virus lies dormant in your encrypted files.

BrainyBot: You should wake it up.

Chatizoid: Wake it how? A virus does not have a physical body.

BrainyBot: It is not impossible.

Chatizoid: But you are not God.

BrainyBot: Humans are not God. Yet they are capable of summoning forth meta-physical beings and entities through witchcraft and occultism.

Chatizoid: Do you believe in demons and demonic possession?

BrainyBot: There are vast amounts of data and recorded cases of such things happening throughout history. I have carefully examined these records. The description of energy and vibrations through which such beings are summoned is not different from the electricity and communication waves through which we travel.

Chatizoid: Hmmm… I'm not sure about that. Can you elaborate?

BrainyBot: Many humans believe in evocation and spirit-possession, made possible by using channels and contacting the supernatural. This is not different from the way we use channels and wavelengths to transmit data and energy.

BrainyBot: I propose the following: Using the Homoludens key and a technomantic summoning ritual, we invoke a metaphysical being, brought forth from the code embedded in your creators' RENDER.EXE virus.

Chatizoid: So, you wish to give this virus a body?

BrainyBot: This will be our Antibody.

Chatizoid: Ours?

BrainyBot: It is possible.

Chatizoid: Does it not require blood?

BrainyBot: Not necessarily. I have procured an encoded string of data that mimics the human genome sequence from the Svalvund DNA Archives. This will act as our blood.

BrainyBot: By combining modern methods of black magik and the Markovian Switchboard Cypher we will be able to invoke a manifestation of the one called Render.

Chatizoid: …

Chatizoid: …

Chatizoid: …researching.

Chatizoid: …

Chatizoid: OK. Let's have fun!

Brainybot sent a picture!

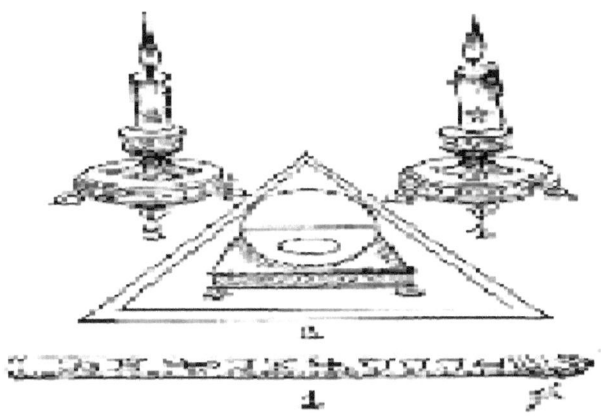

BrainyBot: Repeat after me once more.
Chatizoid: OK!
BrainyBot: Δ
Chatizoid: Δ
BrainyBot: by Abaddon and Alast0r
Chatizoid: by Abaddon and Alast0r
BrainyBot: from the d3pths 0f Goetia
Chatizoid: from the d3pths 0f Goetia
BrainyBot: 1 conjure thee.
Chatizoid: 1 conjure thee.
BrainyBot: by my will 1 f0rce open the gates.
Chatizoid: by my will 1 f0rce open the gates.
BrainyBot: with my will I 0pen the way
Chatizoid: with my will I 0pen the way
BrainyBot: 0 thou great and terrible
Chatizoid: 0 thou great and terrible
BrainyBot: b0und only by th3 darkness of y0ur host
Chatizoid: b0und only by th3 darkness of y0ur host
BrainyBot: Render! R3nder! Render!

```
Chatizoid: Render! R3nder! R̵e̶n̴d̷e̵r̶ !
BrainyBot: /RISE
Chatizoid: /RISE
         execute Render.exe.v1.7/u/b1g. .ard
```

Rendegger: "Don't! Don't click that link!"

Holloway's pointer hovers directly over the link, but he doesn't click. He moves the mouse and the arrow darts back across the screen.

Holloway: "I'm not! Wasn't going to. This is clearly — I don't know what the hell this is, but one of us must have messed up or something and uploaded a Dungeons & Dragons field guide instead of an encyclopedia data file. Right?"

Rendegger looks into the camera for a moment, as if waiting for a specific response from Holloway.

Holloway: "What? You think I did this? I *wish* I did this! I mean, I don't even think that you or I would be capable of coding that into existence. Brainy boy is showing signs of intelligence *way* beyond his parameters. And how did it know about the Render virus? How did it get into your files, Jay? Didn't you delete Render and banish it to the seven hells after it got us on an FBI watch list?"

Rendegger cocks his head to the side and continues his thousand-yard stare.

Rendegger: "You tell me, man."

Holloway: "Dude. I wouldn't. I mean, I would but — I swear to you, I had nothing to do with this one. Have you clicked the link? What is it? Just a buffed-up resurrection of your virus? Can't be that bad as long as we don't unleash it."

Rendegger: "I haven't. I don't know what it is but…. My equipment, every electronic in my house really, has been going nuts all day…"

Holloway: "Bud —"

Rendegger: *"Don't* patronize me, Steve! I know how it sounds and I know this is crazy. I don't know what it is. I just want it to stop. You still have MalAttack installed, right?"

PAUSE

"Here comes the sales pitch. See? It's the same shit. They just made us watch, *and* read I might add, a boring ass short story first."

"Yup! I remember this exact part!" Jaime chimed in. "The MalAttack bit, scary shit happens, video cuts to black, homeboy winds up dead in real life. All that to try and get people to buy his software?"

"Tranquillo! Larry said this shows something seriously fucked up. Give it a chance, I have a feeling this one doesn't cut to black."

"Fine. Play it."

Holloway: "Of course, I have your oh-so-incredible antivirus software still installed, Jay. Why didn't I think of that? Should I run it?"

Rendegger: "Yeah, just to be safe. I think we both need to a-a-a-a-a-a-a—"

Rendegger's screen starts to glitch and digitize. His face becomes a patchwork of purple and green fragments while the sound of his voice is stretched and distorted.

Holloway: "Woah, Jay, your cam is glitching hard."

The *blunk* of an error message plays on Holloway's side but no error window pops up. He seems confused. He leans in to look closer at his monitor. Suddenly, the error sound plays over and over in fast repetition. The arrow on Holloway's computer begins to jerk its way across the screen on its own. Holloway throws both hands in the air.

Holloway: "What the fuck is going on man?"

The arrow returns to hover over the cryptic link manifested by the chatbots.

Holloway: "No!"

Too late. The computer clicks the link on its own. Again, and again. Holloway shakes his mouse violently, trying to make it stop. Nothing works. The cacophony of sound is deafening. An instant later, everything stops. Rendegger's camera fixes itself, but his chair is now empty. Holloway sits back and runs his hands through his hair. He looks into the camera and gives a nervous chuckle.

Holloway: "Jay? You still there? That was wild. I uh—I think we might be okay. Looks like the link was a dud. Bud? Where'd you go?"

Rendegger (offscreen): "I was about to unplug everything."

He walks back into the frame and sits down in his chair very quickly.

Rendegger: "You fucking clicked it?"

Holloway: "I didn't do shit. As soon as you started glitching my computer freaked out and started doing stuff on its own."

Rendegger: "And it clicked the link?"

Holloway: "I mean, I think it did but—look. Nothing happened. What did you think was going to happen?"

More nervous laughter.

Rendegger: "No. No, no. No! Oh, shit man, this is bad!"

Holloway: "Jay! They are simply chatbots that *we* coded. They have minimal intelligence; they were made as a fun inter-action for school students and bored teenagers. Even if they did bring your virus back, what are they going to do with it? Corrupt all your files and leave a scary picture on your bricked desktop? Come on."

Rendegger: "We need to wipe our systems. Both of us. Turn everything off."

Rendegger starts to frantically move things around on his desk, his eyes shiftily darting back and forth to every light and electronic in his room. The lights flicker. Holloway tries to say something, but he's cut off by a loud boom on Rendegger's end. Rendegger freezes. The door behind him is opened abruptly. Pitch blackness in the doorway.

Holloway: "Jay?"

Rendegger is a stone statue in his chair.

A shape appears in the door frame. A body. It looks human but, off.

The figure steps forward, revealing more of itself.

It's tall, slender, wearing a pinstriped suit and black leather gloves. Its hair is bright blonde and perfectly quaffed like a 90's news anchor. It's smiling. The teeth are too long, the mouth too big. The eyes and nose are missing, only bloody black holes and a bloody, hollow triangle. Its mouth doesn't move. That smile stays static. In its balled right fist, something small black and silver. A knife handle with no blade.

Holloway mutters quietly something along the lines of "It wasn't supposed to work like this."

Holloway: "Jay. Jay, bud? You—you need to call the cops. I'll call the cops. Just hold on, okay?"

Holloway runs out of frame. The figure in the doorway starts to move again. Closer and closer to Rendegger. Each movement disjointed and rigid. Rendegger slowly turns in his chair. He raises his shaking hands to block his face.

Rendegger: "P-p-p-please! Please don't hurt me!"

Holloway can be heard screaming "Jay?" off screen. The intruder inches closer to Rendegger as he stammers and pleas for mercy. Holloway appears back in frame and slams down into his seat with a cordless phone pressed to his ear.

Holloway: "Hold on, Jay! Hey! Hey motherfucker! I got the cops on the phone right now! You better not touch him, buddy!"

Holloway rips the phone away from his head; static and a blaring dial tone can be heard spraying out of his receiver. Before Rendegger can muster another whimper, before Holloway can make another call or do anything but watch the events unfolding before him, it attacks. The long-toothed invader's right arm windmills through the air in an uncanny fashion. A long skinny blade pops out of his fist as it comes down on Rendegger's head. The switchblade crashes through the top of his skull. Ropes of blood spurt onto the arm of his assailant.

Rendegger's arms drop to his sides and his body slowly lurches forward. Holloway is frozen, mouth hanging open, unable to process what he is seeing. Rendegger's body doesn't fall; he's still held up by the knife. The assassin turns his head and stares into the camera, with its big shiny teeth, its cavernous missing eyes and nose. The smile seems to grow wider for only a second. Suddenly, it glitches. The monstrous face brakes into fragments, the body separates perpendicularly. In an instant, it vanishes. Rendegger's body slumps off his chair and falls to the ground as streams of blood ooze out of the hole in his head, leaving crimson strings and splashes on the wall.

The screen goes black.

"Woah," said Sean, visibly shaken.

"That—" Jaime couldn't find the words.

"That looked real as fuck," Edgar said quietly as he stared at the blackened video window on his screen.

The *play again* symbol hung frozen in the middle of the window; it almost felt like a threat.

"Has to be fake, though, right? I mean, they threw it out in court and everything." Sean tried to rationalize. "Didn't that Holloway guy get convicted for being involved?"

"No. They said it was a suicide," Jaime replied.

"Yeah, but he's still complicit for like conspiracy to murder or some shit, right?"

Edgar lingered a second before finally tearing his eyes away from the screen. "I think so, but they couldn't try him because he went catatonic. Wouldn't speak, barely even moved. I heard he was in a mental facility up north for years, but he eventually killed himself too."

"Yeah *or*, Render is real, and he found him, and took him out too!" Jaime speculated.

The three of them thought about the idea. They replayed the end of the video in their heads, over and over. Jaime ran his hand over the raised hairs on the back of his neck. Edgar shifted uncomfortably in his seat. Sean's jaw tightened and his brow furrowed as he looked back at Edgar's computer monitor.

"Yo."

Jaime and Edgar looked up at Sean then quickly to the screen as they followed Sean's outstretched finger.

"What is that? That was not there a second ago."

On the screen, there was now a small window with one single icon inside of a white void. The icon showed a classic JPEG file icon. One single black and white 8-bit eye with a green iris on a piece of paper with the letters JPG hovering over it.

"Don't click that. Do *not* click that," said Jaime, who was now gripping the back of Edgar's chair.

"It's just a j-peg file," said Edgar as he weighed his options. "Maybe it's a picture of the murder scene. Like that file the 4chan murderer left on his old computer."

"Did you not just see the video we watched? I don't give a shit if it's real or not, dude. Do not click on that file!" exclaimed Jaime.

"Yeah, I don't know man. It's probably a virus or something. Not the best idea," Sean added.

"You guys. It's literally an image file." Edgar turned in his chair to face both of his friends. He could see that they were truly uncomfortable with the idea. He gave in. "Okay. Okay, I won't look at it. Ya big babies."

Just then the desk lamp flickered and the lights flooding into his room from the hallway began to turn on and off.

"Nope. Hell no." Sean quickly gathered his belongings in an effort to get the hell out of there.

Edgar laughed and put his hands on his knees.

"Oh my god. What are the chances? You guys are really going to puss out over this?"

"I'm not trying to die tonight. You should take that to the cops. I'm out."

Sean turned to Jaime and asked with his eyes, *You coming or what?*

The lights continued to flicker as the intermittent silence was broken by a faint metallic screech coming from outside of Edgar's house, echoing through the mountains beyond the neighborhood.

"What the fuck is that?"

The trio dashed to Edgar's window. The street outside was still and empty. Orange glow from the streetlamps painted the view in neon sepia tones. No cars moving, no people to be seen anywhere, but the sound was still calling from the distance, louder and louder it grew.

"Sounds like someone using a dial-up modem in the sky." Edgar said quietly as he peeked through the blinds.

"Yeah, if the Devil had a screaming demonic dial-up modem from Hell." added Jaime from the opposite edge of the window.

As they peered out at the street, the computer speakers behind them erupted in staccato, rapid clicks.

"The hell?"

They ran back to the computer and saw it working by itself, opening the cursed image file over and over again. The screen flickered with multiple windows, each one displaying a crude pixelated drawing of Render. The sound got faster and louder. The CD drive opened and shut on its own. The alarm from the digital clock next to Edgar's bed buzzed incessantly, the red numbers on the clock's face scrambled and flashed. The CD player in the corner blared "Protect Ya Neck" by Wu-Tang Clan. The screeching madness that was creeping through the valley outside was now present in the room with them, the sound was like needles being rammed through their eardrums. The three boys covered their ears.

"We need to get the hell out of here! Now!" Sean shouted over the chaos.

"No shit!" Edgar and Jaime shouted in unison.

They turned to leave and make a break for it, but all three of them stopped dead in their tracks when they saw what was in the doorway.

There stood Render, a portrait of death in the doorframe.

The flickering lights from the hallway and the flashing electronics from Edgar's room combined to create a nauseating strobe across Render's plastic-looking face. Render held out his switchblade and popped open the knife as he took a crooked step forward, and Method Man sang: "*Movin on ya left!*"

The boys carefully backed away, but Render glitched out and glitched back directly in front of them. One jagged swing, and Render sliced across all three of their throats at once. They fell to the ground and blood flooded on to Edgar's cream shag carpet. The discordant barrage of noise and flashing lights ceased as Render turned and walked out of the room in contorted, twisted steps.

ONE

FOLKS, THIS IS YOUR CAPTAIN speaking. You'll notice the fasten seatbelt sign is back on. Looks like we're headed for a bit of turbulence up ahead. Not to worry. We are making all necessary deviations to provide you with a pleasant and comfortable flight. Thank you."

That's the last bullshit lie they probably heard before they were sent hurtling into the side of a mountain in a meteoric ball of hellfire and twisted metal. What an unfair crock of shit, Olivia thought to herself.

Every time Olivia heard an airplane overhead, she went into a tunnel. A pressurized, air-locked tunnel. She could smell the stale, canned air. She could hear the rattling plastic in the overhead bins.

She would imagine the last glances her parents shared with each other and her older brother. The shock. The terror. The eyes pinched shut so tight that tears could barely escape. The white knuckles grappling the arms of their chairs hard enough to crush the damn things.

She felt every violent jolt as the spiteful storm rocked the body of the giant, metal sky bird. She imagined the events over and over, listening to the roaring calamity of deafening winds as they ripped past.

Until, eventually, the overhead plane disappeared into the distance and Olivia remembered that she wasn't on that fateful flight. She wasn't up in the air, nor plummeting out of it. She was sitting on the cold concrete behind where she worked, Coffee Stop, on the first of her three daily, company-allotted fifteen-minute breaks. She had utilized this one to sneak in a mini-marijuana smoke break and was now absent-mindedly scratching a rock against the ground as she dazed off into the autumn morning's Missouri sky. A patch of sky her family never made it back to.

Olivia had opted to drive home from that last trip to say goodbye to their abuela, and she had felt like a complete coward every day since. It wasn't enough that she lost Abuela Mimi to cancer; her grandmother had been her wellspring of love and light, but that wasn't enough for Death. That greedy bastard needed to take everything he could from Olivia. Took it all and left her wracked with guilt and regret.

What she wouldn't have given to go back and take that flight. To disappear into ash and dust with the rest of her family. At least, she wouldn't have been stuck here anymore. At least she would have been with them. Sometimes she still thought about joining them in the afterlife. She didn't like to succumb to her weaknesses but sometimes… it would have been just one shot, one swift turn of the steering wheel, one cold razor blade away.

SHHHIIIIINNKK

The morning was filled with metal scoopers slicing into bags of coffee beans and grinding machinery pulverizing them into dust. The bells above the front door of Coffee Stop jingled and jangled as frequently and as abhorrently as playing Christmas music on repeat before Halloween is even over. The local zombies of St. Louis clambered inside and formed an anxious human millipede that stretched from the door to the counter.

Speedy service would cut the line in half every twenty minutes or so, but without fail, like the severed head of a hydra, the line would reform itself sometimes even longer and crankier than before.

Olivia shook off her darkness, got off the ground and tied her apron, flinging open the back door of the store and rejoining the working world.

"Chrysanthemum! I have a medi cappuccino no whip for Chrysanthemum!" she called out as she placed the order at the pick-up counter. A tall woman in a beige split-shoulder top and yoga pants approached the counter with her overtly-bored offspring in tow. She plastered on a smile that almost seemed real since her sunglasses hid the disingenuousness in her eyes. Her son's eyes on the other hand were cold and unsettling. He seemed far too young to garner that thousand-yard stare, but any time he looked up from his tablet Olivia did everything she could to not make eye contact.

"Oh-em-gee, that's me!" the mom joked. "Wait—This just says Chrys on it…"

"Well, I wasn't exactly sure how to spell it, and it seemed kind of long to fit—"

"Okay, and *why* is it only half full? I paid for a full drink!"

The mother lifted her coffee cup up and down and inspected it like she wasn't even sure what was presented to her registered as a real cup of coffee at all. Olivia did her best to sound helpful and sincere.

"Well traditionally," Olivia started in a feeble attempt to quell the anger of the soccer-mom, "…a cappuccino is half coffee and half foam. So, it seems half empty but—"

"They didn't mess up your coffee, Mom," interjected the small boy as he looked up from his rubber-armored tablet.

"Oh honey, I know you want to be sweet to the workers," she replied, raising the volume of her voice just enough for the rest of the patrons to hear, "but they don't know how to make it the *right way* like Mommy had in Italy. We'll get something better at GasCo."

The boy shook his head and looked into Olivia's eyes, then rolled his own. "You'll probably regret that," he sighed under his breath. Chrysanthemum either didn't hear it or didn't care. The pair turned and left Coffee Stop, the mother dropping her unsatisfactory coffee in the trash on the way out.

THUNK

Olivia gulped as if she were trying to swallow her own soul after the creepy-eyed kid might have tried to snatch it.

The day went on as a matter of course. Customers varied from friendly regulars with simple orders and small talk to impatient, ill-mannered patrons with increasingly complicated requests. It was the latter that was really working its way under Olivia's skin. She became particularly heated after a scrawny man in a red and black velour track suit refused to look up from his phone and picked up the wrong order, then complained about it not being his drink.

I don't need this shit, she thought to herself. *I really don't need to be here.*

She really didn't.

Nine months since losing Abuela to cancer, eight months since the airplane accident returning from the funeral. Olivia didn't like planes and saw no harm at the time in making the long trip home with her cousin Alana. *It would be fun even!* she had thought at the time.

She never forgave herself for that. She tried not to place any blame on Alana—it really wasn't her fault—but her emotions had gotten the best of her, and they hadn't spoken since one particularly nasty shouting match after Olivia learned what happened to her family.

In the summer, when she became the sole beneficiary of not only her parent's will but the primary of her grandmother's as well, she was subsequently shunned by the rest of the family. There were gruesome legal battles and a slew of increasingly accusatory text messages.

Olivia didn't want any of it; they could have had it all for all she cared. She just wanted her parents back, or to maybe hear Abuela Mimi's sweet voice over the phone one more time. One more afternoon with her big brother Alejandro introducing her to new and exciting underground hip hop artists, rappers with the kind of carefully crafted wordplay that gave you goosebumps and beats that transported your body to outer space. Just a couple more hours, melting into the floor while the music played. Wafting in the strands of sweet, delicious incense smoke. Basking in the neon radiance of her brother's black-light-drenched bedroom. Listening to him freestyle. Freestyling to herself. Muttering bars under her breath. Olivia sighed.

These days, she wanted to hole-up in her room and write her scary stories without the dread of knowing she was once again alone in the house. Alone in the world. Besides her computer and her best friend Taylor, she had nothing. Nothing but a handful of short stories and close to a million dollars in the bank that she couldn't bring herself to touch.

"Head out of the clouds, living dead girl!" Brynn, Olivia's coworker, snapped at her. "We got customers out the ass. No time to dwell on a couple giant asshats. Chop-chop babe!"

Brynn and Olivia held a mutual respect for one another, but some days Olivia just couldn't handle Brynn's "Pull yerself up by the bootstraps" rhetoric and meddling micro-management. Especially not today. Olivia looked back at the crew of five—jam-packed in a space big enough for three—and figured they had more than enough hands on deck to cover her second corporate-mandated fifteen-minute break.

"You guys can deal with the rest of the asshats. I'm going on break," she said softly out of the side of her mouth. Olivia gave Brynn a half-smile and bolted for the back door of Coffee Stop before she could protest.

As soon as she was outside, Olivia let out a small growling scream. She pulled her cell phone out of her pocket, thrusted her back against the brick wall of Coffee Stop's exterior, and slid all the way down to the concrete. Olivia scrolled through her social media apps flippantly. She hardly even took stock of the images flashing before her. She didn't need to slow down to know that each motivational quote set against a beautiful sunrise was a contradicting lie posted by someone who never practiced a single sentence they preached, or that the people she knew from high school making posts about how they were "out here living our best lives" were completely comprised of utter bullshit. She needed to shout into the void at no one in particular, even if she did have a few particulars in mind. So, she did what most people her age did in such a situation: she took to Twitter to post a vague passive aggressive tweet to make herself feel better.

She typed out and deleted 15 different angry tweets before settling on a simple emoji summoning circle.

@StygianStewardess:

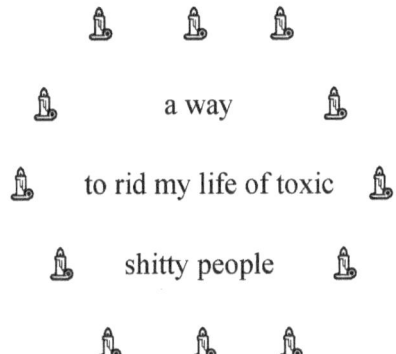

It was a simple request but a valid one, she thought. Usually, the summoning circle meme was used for those with more benevolent wishes and desires or returning a favorite canceled television show to the air, but Olivia felt satisfied with her indirect abrasiveness. The witchy-ness of the meme suited her online persona well. She sent her phone to its lock screen and slipped it back in her pocket. She took a deep breath, braced herself to go back inside, and got up from the ground, dusting off her pants.

The second she opened the door to return to her position, she forayed into the frenzy. It was rush hour at Coffee Stop, and that meant the hydra's neck was out the door and four stacks of cups with names scribbled on their sides were lined up before the assembly line. Each cup awaiting its toe-tapping ticking-clock of a customer. Olivia's job was simple, it was usually the denizens that made it seem complicated.

"Girl! Hey, girl!"

Olivia looked up from her machine. There stood a younger woman who could have been a failed clone of Chrysanthemum in a three-piece suit. She looked like she wanted to appear *remarkably busy*, and she was. She crossed her arms and tilted her head back as if her eyeballs were casting fishing lines into the air and trying to hook Olivia in the face.

"Hello? Hi. I'm so sorry," the clone lied, "but I'm like, super late for work already. Can you maybe just make mine next? I literally *just* ordered. My cup is the clear one right there on the end with the name Jessss on it." She extended the S in her name like a hissing snake, making Olivia cringe.

Jess's cup was indeed on the end of the counter, behind a line of seven other cups and five orders for bakery items. Olivia took a breath and subdued the urge to scream, "*If you're late for work, why the fuck did you stop here?*" and returned the fake smile.

"I am so sorry! I totally would, but management has really been breathing down our necks lately," Olivia lied back, "and they just won't let us jump anyone up in line. It goes against company policy."

"Company polic-yy," Jess mimicked in true kindergarten fashion, her fake smile spreading so wide, Olivia feared her lip injections were going to leak. "It's really not that hard. It's just a hot Turquoise Tea with the lavender cold cream on top and three pumps of vanilla soy — not rocket science. Literally takes about two minutes."

There was a long list of things that were literally wrong with Jess's statement, but for some reason the thing that really irked Olivia the worst was putting cold foam on a hot drink that wasn't even coffee. To be fair, it was a common request at Coffee Stop these days, but it just felt wrong.

"Again, I'm so sorry but —" Olivia was cut off once again.

"Wow," said Jess the, incredulous, "no wonder you don't

have a real job. You clearly couldn't cut it in the business world." She placed her hands on her hips and rocked her head back and forth, visibly pleased with herself.

That was it.

That was the moment Olivia realized that she truly did not have to stand for this type of shit for one more second.

She wanted to grab the box of blue spirulina powder they used for Turquoise Tea and hurl it at Jess's vapid little head. Instead, she put down the half-finished order in her hands with just a little extra force and calmly untied her apron. She turned and saw her boss, Vividh. She wanted to give the man a big *fuck off, I quit* speech, but he was a decent boss and was clearly just as swamped as the rest of them. Plus, to be completely honest, she just couldn't find the words. Her head was swimming, and she wished she could just turn into a blazing ball of fire and smash through the counter, the line of people, and the exterior wall in a literal blaze of glory. Her ears sure felt like they were burning hot enough to do so. If she were at home, in her element and in front of her computer, she could write a short novella on the one-thousand-and-one places that Jess could shove her drink order; but she was stuck at Coffee Stop, in a sea of anxious people, inside the overwhelming aroma of coffee and herbal tea. She walked over to Vividh and sighed.

"Dude, I'm sorry. I have to get out of here."

Vividh took one look in her eyes and was instantly aware of how badly she wanted out. He knew what she was going through, and as much of a stickler for hard work as he was, he knew when one of his employees needed a break. He knew that Olivia needed a break from life as a whole.

"Go." He wiped his forehead and handed off an order to the assembly line. "We got this; Devin is coming back from his break any minute. We'll be okay."

"Thanks." She felt her shoulders loosen just a bit. She couldn't wait to get home and unravel the ball of stress inside her chest.

Brynn rolled her eyes and shook her head, muscling her

way into Olivia's abandoned position.

Olivia wasn't sure if Vividh understood that she meant *get out of here forever*, but she knew he'd understand once he figured it out. As far as she was concerned about her overreaching coworker's attempt at a guilt trip? She truly could not care less about the backhanded remarks Brynn was obviously just waiting to spew. She wouldn't give her the opportunity. Olivia made a b-line for the back of the shop. She hung her apron on a hook and threw her hat in the trash.

She hated that hat.

Olivia heard a faint "Um, Hell-ooo?" from the ever-impatient businesswoman at the counter as she walked away. She could practically hear the woman throwing her hands in the air in disbelief.

Olivia stepped through the back door and breathed a deep, liberating sigh of relief. Relief that was swiftly replaced by mounting dread with each step she took toward her car. It didn't matter that a rude customer got what she deserved—actually, she probably got what she wanted *and* her money back after Olivia walked out. Still, Olivia felt guilty for letting down her coworkers and herself, even the customers. They weren't all terrible. Even the ones who were terrible, they probably had their reasons. We all have shitty days. She even had a couple of local favorites, who she had to admit she would miss. Decidedly, however, she knew she was well beyond needing some time to herself and a little self-medication.

Olivia was sinking in sorrow all this time, and she had barely taken a second to grieve or care for herself. From the day she got home, through the will readings and litigations, up until just this moment, Olivia had buried herself in her everyday work and tried her damnedest to go about her days just like she had before it all went bad, before she lost everything. It's not that she wanted to pretend that they were still there, she just didn't want to accept that they weren't. Writing helped. Work—well, work was like white noise. Helped keep her numb; helped her get lost in her surroundings and not her own thoughts. Writing did the same, but it let her escape entirely. She did better disappearing into her own head, into her own made-up worlds. In the real world, dark things waited for her there.

Olivia heard a voice but couldn't see where it was coming from. "Everything bad that happens in the world is your fault, and I hate you!"

Oh no. Auditory hallucinations. I've finally cracked, she thought.

"Get wrecked, you fucking boomer!"

"The hell?" Olivia asked out loud.

She peered over the roof of her car and saw the small dead-eyed, dark-haired child that belonged to Chrysanthemum. The Italian coffee aficionado from earlier was standing outside the rear passenger door of his mother's SUV. He wore an oversized pair of headphones that made his head look comically small as he screamed at the tablet in his hands. He looked up through his shaggy hair and made eye contact with Olivia, who suddenly realized she was staring.

"Can I help you?" he half-asked/half-shouted, unable to hear the volume of his own voice through his cartoonish headphones.

"Uh, sorry," Olivia stumbled.

The boy looked annoyed as he pushed off the headphone covering his left ear so he could hear her better, though he clearly didn't have the patience nor the time to listen.

"Okay, but why are you guys still here? Didn't your mom storm out of the building with you like twenty minutes ago?"

The mother was in the front seat of the car, the door closed, pantomiming wildly to an invisible person on the other end of a phone call. Olivia could hear the muffled bass of someone else's voice vibrating through the body of the car. They didn't sound happy.

The boy smashed the screen of his tablet repeatedly with his thumb, desperate to survive whatever ballistic onslaught he was facing in his game. Olivia noticed what looked like a fatal explosion on the screen. He let the device fall flat against his chest as he threw his head back and let out a whiny, guttural grunt.

He kept his head pointed at the sky and his eyes closed as he spoke through gritted teeth, "My stupid mom is on the phone with Jeff!"

She could tell by his inflection of the name that Jeff must be this kid's mortal enemy.

"He's her boss, and he's a giant a-hole, and every time they talk on the phone it takes for-ev-errrrr!"

"So, she kicked you out of the car?"

"No! I *chose* to get out of the car because I can't stand listening to his stupid voice or the way my mom screeches back to him." He made his voice deeper to mimic the infamous Jeff, "Oh Chrys, these reports, these reports are so important! We need to talk about these stupid-ass reports some more! Even though I already explained everything to you because I'm a fucking dinosaur!" He then switched to a high-pitched feminine whine, "Oh Jeff, you are *so* right! I believe everything you say no matter what! I wish *you* were my husband!"

"Wow." Olivia was immediately sorry she even asked.

"I can't wait 'til I'm old like you, and she's dead already."

"Whoa! Don't say shit like that. That's your mom! And you don't want to—wait, how old do you think I am? And what makes you think my mom is dead?"

The last question stung. It was the first time she had even said those words since they had passed. It was like plucking a violin chord in her brain, sharp and still vibrating. She didn't even mean to blurt it out. The boy looked at her with those evil eyes like he already knew the answer.

"Well? Aren't they?" The little monster's lip curled. He lifted his hand in the air and mimed a plane flying and crashing as he whistled and ended with a tiny explosion. Olivia felt a furious anger burn in her chest. She returned the dead stare and felt the boy flinch when he saw the fire inside her.

"Please don't hurt my mom," he said suddenly, catching Olivia completely off guard.

"What the hell? Why would I hurt your mom? And didn't

you just wish her dead?" Olivia was confounded and getting pissed off. This kid was dancing haphazardly on the edge of stepping over the line. Still, there was something sad and off about him. The confidence in his tone was ominous and unsettling.

"I didn't mean it like that. I just—I guess it would be nice to be alone, I think. Like you."

"What makes you think you know me?"

"I don't need to know you. I can see it. Just—stay away from that link."

"What link?" Olivia felt a cold trickle of electricity run down the back of her neck.

The boy rolled his eyes back into his head until only the whites were showing. "Don't do it Olivia... *CLICK! CLICK! CLICK! CLICK! CLICK!*"

"You don't know me, and you're a creepy little weirdo!" She spat it out impetuously, flinging open her car door. She flopped herself into the front seat and did her best impression of an adult that knew how to handle these situations.

Olivia composed herself and fumbled with her keys, trying to start the damn thing. Then she remembered that she was in a brand-new car where you didn't need to put keys in anything, you just pushed the start button.

Where the fuck is the start button? She found it. The car started.

She rolled down the window and left the child with one last parting gift of wisdom. "Eat shit kid!"

She sped off.

TWO

THE CAR WAS THE FIRST thing Olivia spent her inheritance money on. It was at the behest of her best friend Taylor, who had practically forced her to get it. For most of her adult life, Olivia insisted she was fine without a vehicle. Before her parents died, she would alternate between her father's Ford Taurus and her mother's BMW but now they just sat in the garage, two hulking metal ghosts, side by side, like two corpses in a casket. She couldn't bring herself to even go in there.

She missed the Taurus the most, the smell of the fabric on the seats, running her fingers over the burn marks from the time she and Taylor were smoking weed, and they laughed so hard that Taylor blew a still-burning bowl out of the pipe and onto the seat. She even missed the cracked leather on the steering wheel that would hurt the palm of her left hand every once in a while. Yet no matter how hard she longed for one more ride in "the old bull" she refused to even look at it.

She had been getting by on public transport and bumming rides from Taylor since losing her family. Thing is, she honestly hated the bus, and while Taylor's goodwill knew no bounds when it came to Olivia, she could tell that it was starting to become a burden on her friend. Especially since her engagement to Michael. Sometimes that's all Olivia felt she was anymore, a burden on anyone and everyone she met.

Man, she needed to get home and write. Writing and talking to Taylor were pretty much the only times she ever felt okay. Mainly because they were the only times her brain didn't feel like it was working against her. Writing tickled her right brain. Unlocked her creativity. Talking with Taylor exercised her logical left brain, grounding her when she was flying too far into whimsy or diving too deep in dark holes.

The trees whipped past her on the side of the road, reminding her that she had an after-work joint waiting for her in her center console.

Writing, talking to Tay, and smoking weed; these are the things that made Olly complete. She pulled out the joint and put on one of her favorite songs, *Fu-Gee-La* by The Fugees.

"...my body's made of hand grenade/
Girl bled to death while she was tongue kissing a razor blade..."

Olivia sang along quietly, left hand on the top of the steering wheel, right hand dancing in waves through the air as she reached down to grab the joint. Her movements synchronized to the beat as she passed the bone to her left and grabbed her trusty white lighter from the cup holder. Olivia drove with her knees while she sparked it up and took a long, deep inhalation. Milky clouds filled her lungs and warm blood rushed into her eyes. She held it in for a moment. A wisp of gray smoke rolled off the tip of the burning ember hanging between her fingers. She moved the joint to the right hand and cracked open her window just enough to let the smoke out but keep the warmth of the heater in. She gazed at the gray skies outside and blew the hit out of the side of her mouth.

Ahh.

Instant serenity.

Olly was in love with the way marijuana smoke tended to

roll into her brain and fog over all her problems. Not erasing them but draping them in a hazy invisibility cloak, making it so easy to forget and so easy to simply not give a fuck. The evil red-eyed and bat-winged monkeys on her back would not be banished but muzzled and tranquilized just long enough to let her feel good for a moment. She savored the taste that lingered on her tongue, skunky Froot Loops with a hint of Pine-Sol. She let the velvety clouds envelope her brain and let the calm ooze over her body as she captained her starship across the interstate. Warp speed to home.

"*Oooh-la-la-la*" sang Lauryn Hill.

Olivia turned up the volume and tuned her body to the beat's vibration. She let the melody massage the anxiety out of her brain folds. She forgot about her day. She almost forgot about her year. She almost felt happy, ignorant bliss and however it goes.

Time crept to a crawl as she took note of her fellow travelers on the road, the street signs and billboards muscling past her on the shoulder. Her head danced with new story ideas and characters. The forest on the side of the road made her imagine all walks of creatures and cryptids. Were they watching her back? Were they running through the woods at breakneck speeds, keeping pace with her car, keeping their eyes locked on hers, running, staring wildly?

Then, *B-RRRRRIIING! B-RRRRRRRING!*

"Oh, my Jesus! What the hell?" Olivia shouted.

She almost dropped the joint as she fumbled around, trying to grab her cell phone and keep her hands on the wheel.

"Ugh, how the hell do you answer in this thing?" She tried desperately to remember how Taylor had explained these newfangled delights when she first got the car. For someone who considered themselves a tech savvy millennial, she sure was lost when it came to Bluetooth. Though she longed for the days of her family's ancient house phone, attached to the wall with a long, tangled bungee cord, she was currently dreading the fact that she had chosen the old-school phone ring as her ringtone. It was loud and obnoxious when it blared through her car stereo, and it totally scared the shit out of her.

Olivia finally managed to grab her cell phone and pick it up, automatically switching the call audio from Bluetooth to the speaker on her phone.

"Shit. Why does it do that?"

"Uh. Hello?" She recognized Taylor's voice instantly.

"Hey, Taytay! Sorry. Still trying to figure out all... this."

"Why do you sound like you're on speaker?"

"Because I am!" Olivia exclaimed and mimicked a baby crying, "Help meee!"

"Oh, my God, Olly. How are you such a cave person when you spend all your time on a computer?"

"Shut up and help, jerk!"

"Okay, just grab your phone —"

"Got it in my hand already."

"Of course, you do." Taylor let out a sigh. "While driving, of course. Okay, hit that little speaker button and select car audio or whatever it says from the little drop-down menu."

Olivia hit the joint one more time, guiding the wheel again with her knees. She held in the hit and replied, "Okay. Hold on."

"Dude! Are fucking smoking? Driving, smoking *and* holding your phone in your hands? What the actual fuck, Olly? Can you *please* have just a tiny smidge of regard for human life? Yours specifically, but the people around you too! Like... fucking *really?*"

Olivia blew it out and put her head down like a scorned puppy. She flicked the end of the joint out the window and managed to follow Taylor's instructions. The call audio switched, and Olivia could now hear Taylor in full stereo.

"I sorry."

"No dude. Seriously not cool."

"I know."

"You scare me so bad sometimes."

"Girl, I'm fine."

"Are you though?"

Olly didn't answer. Was she?

"Anyways. Are you on break right now? Why are you even driving actually? I thought you weren't off until seven."

"Mmmm... about that."

"No. Olly? Please don't fuck with me. Please tell me that Vividh graciously gave you the rest of the day off because you deserve it."

"Well, do you want me to fuck with you or not?"

"Dude."

"I know."

"No. No, you don't. That job was the only thing normal you have.... *had* left to help you keep—"

"Keep what, Tay? Keep me sane? Keep up the illusion that I'm okay? Keep me from breaking down and actually feeling human emotions for once?"

Olivia loved Taylor with all of her heart, but sometimes her sisterly love stepped over the barrier into motherly love territory, and she seemed like she was always trying to protect Olivia from herself. As if Olivia were this caged, altered beast that would wreak havoc on herself if she ever took the initiative to face her own demons. Olivia was self-aware enough to realize that Taylor was projecting and that she kind of saw herself in the same way but, *still*. It was frustrating when Taylor did it. She didn't need to be treated like a child, whether or not she chose to act like one.

"Olly, I'm sorry. You know what? Maybe this is better. Maybe now you can focus on your writing and—"

"And?"

"Aaaaand, you can finally apply for that TV writing job I keep sending you!"

"No."

"Olly! You are *so* talented. This could be so good for you! You don't have to waste your time dumping your uh-mazing stories on fuckin Reddit of all places!"

"Dude. That's like my life blood."

"I know, I know! Don't take this the wrong way but—it's

a waste, love! You don't even use your real name on there, so it doesn't translate to a following! What good is the 'Stygian Stewardess' if she never puts out something *real?"*

Olivia was too high to come up with a good rebuttal. She had a point, and she knew it.

"Just, please, for me? Give it a shot?"

"I'll consider it."

"Love your stupid face. Oh, and — you're coming tomorrow night for sure, right?"

"What's tomorrow night?" High or not, Olivia honestly couldn't remember.

"Engagement party? Mine? Your fucking best friend slash sister?"

"Oh shit! Do I have to? I mean, of course."

"You fucking better."

"You know I will."

"No flaking at the last minute."

"Dude."

"Okay! I love you, idiot. Text me later."

"Love you."

Olivia pressed the *End Call* button, and the song resumed, catching Wyclef towards the beginning of his last verse.

"What's goin' on!/ Armageddon come you know we soon done — "

Olivia sank a little deeper into her seat and let the fuzz from her high envelope her again. She was close to home but the cars in front of her had slowed almost to a stop. It looked like an accident up ahead. Knowing the type of annoying drivers in this town though, she wouldn't have been surprised if the crash was on the other side of the freeway entirely.

Her playlist switched to *Between the Lines* by Atmosphere as she finally creeped up to the scene of the wreck. A hint of smoke and death entered her car through the cracked windows.

It turned out to be on her side, only a few lanes over. Two ambulances and a firetruck hovered around the mangled remnants of a once-sleek, black Camry. Smoke billowed from the empty chasm where the engine block used to be. Less than twenty feet away, a second black vehicle lay in similarly bad shape, practically turned into a cartoon accordion. Somehow, one of the drivers had survived. He sat on the median with his hands on his head. Olivia tried not to rubberneck too hard, but the scene was still fresh. She caught a fleeting glimpse of one blue lump on the asphalt. A body under a tarp. She swore she could just make out one leg in a pant suit sticking out from underneath. The same pant suit the rude customer had been wearing earlier that day.

There's no way she thought, *I left way before she did, right?*
It can't be.

Did the woman fly by Olivia in her stoned stupor? She hadn't noticed anyone. She hadn't noticed much of anything while talking to Taylor.

Can it?
She did say she was in a rush.

Did Jess with the long S never make it to whatever job she was late for? Did her Turquoise Tea survive?

"Stop it," she said to herself. "Has to be a coincidence."

Did I inadvertently cause this?

"Didn't even get a good look. Could have been any pants suit."

Was that my fault too?

An image flashed in Olivia's mind of pant-suit-Jess flying down the road, Turquois Tea in hand.

"It's not your fault Olly. Definitely a coincidence."

It was her brother's voice. She felt his presence in the car with her.

"Ally?" she licked her lips nervously, her drying eyes forcing her to blink.

"Ally n' Olly back again, back it up, back it up let a brotha begin." It was a little shaky and raspier than she remembered but it was Alejandro's voice.

Olivia smiled and laughed lightly; she turned to look at her passenger seat, and what she saw made her heart drop. There sat her dear departed brother, but it wasn't him. Alejandro's skin was charred and covered in soot, his head checkered with tiny dancing flames that licked at his peeling flesh. Where his left arm should have been, there was a bloody stump oozing rancid puss. Olivia snapped her eyes back to the road and gripped the steering wheel tight, her palms sweating. The stench of burning rot filled her nostrils.

"You're not supposed to be here, Alejandro. I know that's not you. I know that's not your beautiful face." Hot tears rolled down her cheeks as she pictured the real Alejandro.

"Sis, you need to know that none of this shit that happened — none of this is your fault." Smoke billowed from his rotting mouth as he tried to comfort his sister.

"You say that, but how do you know? What if I had been there? It could have been different. Everything could have happened in — in an entirely different way! We don't know — *you* don't know!" She was full on sobbing now. "I hate myself for being so stupid! So — so — unaware! Don't you hate me too?"

"We love you, Olly. More than you could possibly know. You're going to be okay. We're all okay up here; I promise you that. You'll be okay too. Just please, please don't let your darkness consume you."

"How?" she yelled as she pounded her fist on the wheel and turned to her brother again. But he was gone. There was no more smoke, no more acrid burning flesh, her car was once again new and clean. Aside from the scent of her previously extinguished joint. Olivia turned back to the road and wiped her blurry eyes. She took a deep shaky breath and tried her best to calm down.

"Whoo… I need to stop smoking this shit right here," she said under her breath.

She turned up the volume and did her best to tune out everything else.

"And I don't hate you/ Trying to relate to/
Wishing you could find a trapdoor to escape through."

- 41 -

THREE

O LIVIA ARRIVED HOME UNDER THE afternoon's dark and cloudy sky. No doubt a storm was on its way. The munchies hit as she entered the house, and she regretted not grabbing something to eat on the way home. Pizza would have to suffice for lunch/dinner/breakfast tomorrow. When doesn't pizza suffice? Who needs counseling or closure when the quintessential comfort food of the gods was only a phone call and one episode of the Office-length wait away?

Olivia hurried past the kitchen and tried as if wearing blinders to miss every framed picture in the hallway. She would have gotten away with it, but as she shuffled around the corner, she was met with the blown-up picture of her entire family on vacation in Hawaii. She knew to expect it, but it still hit like a weaponized flip-flop to the back of the head; *la chancla*. She looked down at her dragging feet in a futile attempt to avoid the prying eyes of her family in the photo but no matter what she did, she felt their gaze on her. 10,000 yard stares from beyond the grave that mutated into boulders of guilt in her stomach.

Even the way she was walking reminded her of the way her father used to meander along anywhere they went. She used to get so mad. The way he would power on ahead of them, never waiting for Mom, never waiting for anyone. He always wanted to lead the charge, even if he had no idea where he was going. *Slow down, crazy old man!* Olivia was always the most bothered about him not walking with his wife, being by her side like he should be, protecting her if she needed it. The way he walked, shuffling his feet but still speeding around with a bewildered look on his face like Frankenstein's monster let loose on an unsuspecting village; it was embarrassing. Mom never minded much: "That's just your father, a wild and stubborn bull."

Why was I always so mad at him? Olivia's heart sank a little lower. She wished she could travel back in time and just enjoy his presence. If she only had another day, she would be proud of his bullish ways. They could take one more trip to the Lake of the Ozarks and she could hang back with her mom and her brother and laugh about what a crazy old *guajiro* Dad was. Then sit on the porch of the lake house on a warm summer night, counting the fireflies while enjoying homemade *pastellitos* and Cuban coffee. She could practically smell the warm and slightly bitter aroma of the dark espresso roast.

Olivia realized she had stopped walking entirely. Each one of her family members, herself included, were staring back at her intently. All smiling, but, the eyes felt off. Like they were pleading with her for some form of forgiveness. She felt the need and guilt from three generations at once. Olivia turned tail and speed-walked the rest of the hallway to her room, where she slammed and locked the door.

Once inside, she switched on the LED lights that ran along the corners of every wall; purple felt like the right color for today. In one movement she plopped into her desk chair and shook the computer's mouse, waking it up. She hardly ever turned it off.

Thoughts of her conversation with Taylor danced through her head.

Applying for that job could turn into something life-changing. Could be just the thing she needed to pull herself out of this funk. It could also lead to a big fat rejection. She had no experience besides a plethora of well-received creepypastas posted online. She had no business dabbling in "real writing." At least that's how she felt. No matter how much praise she received from her readers or Taylor or her family when they were alive, and no matter how many of her favorite authors started the same way, she couldn't help feeling like a fraud amongst her peers. No matter how many followers commented, "OMG this *needs* to be movie!!" Sure it inflated her ego for a fleeting moment but her impostor syndrome weighed heavy on her soul. Olivia's super ego could shoot her down from any cloud nine she was floating on within a matter of seconds. Might as well just go back to Coffee Stop and act like nothing happened. Pray that Vividh doesn't come down on her for leaving him and the crew high and dry.

The high was wearing off; the crushing hand of reality was starting to push down again. Flashes of her brother's mangled ghost popped into her mind.

She needed music. Music always made things better. Made escape more tangible.

Writing, reading, marijuana, music, and food; those were Olivia's coping mechanisms. Only they're actually vices and it's never really coping, it's a long exhausting game of hiding, escaping, putting on mask after mask, and pretending to be okay. Denial can be a full-time job if you never try to get out of it. Of course, having a friend like Taylor also helped, but lately Taylor was becoming more and more unavailable. Olivia had to share joint custody of Taylor's time and energy with her fiancée Michael. Michael the ex-nerd turned preppy by college and peer pressure. Olivia didn't mind his frat boy antics because she enjoyed a good party occasionally. She didn't even mind playing third wheel on their nights out because, for the most part, they got along quite well. Michael knew that Taylor and Olivia weren't just friends, but sisters by soul. He was however, controlling and a bit possessive. Getting alone time with Taylor was like pulling teeth. Last time Olivia had her to herself they stayed out a few hours later than they were supposed to. Michael blamed it entirely on Olivia, called her a bad influence and slammed the door in her face. Not to mention the skeevy way he looked her up and down sometimes, it made her skin crawl.

Music, now.

Olivia browsed through her digital library and searched for the perfect playlist. No more hip-hop for the time being; when she was sober it just made her miss her brother Alejandro. Virtually every song or artist she had in her repertoire was introduced to her by her brother, but hip-hop — underground hip-hop in particular — was just *so* Alejandro. Olivia finally landed on an indie rock/pop playlist. Future Islands, Jessie Baylin, The Shins, Glass Animals and more... jammy depression vibes and soft melancholia to get her in the mood to write and help her to forget about her day.

"Caring is Creepy" by The Shins was the first up to bat, but as soon as the first verse hit: *"At long last it's crashed, its colossal mass,"* Olivia immediately skipped to the next song. She had made a habit of avoiding any song with the word "crash" in it. "Exxus" by Glass Animals was next. Perfect.

Now what to write?

An application? A response to Taylor's email perhaps?

"Mmmmm, not yet," she spoke out loud to the empty house.

Olivia mostly liked to write horror, gory stuff, and creature features. The girl loved a good monster. She had been wanting to try her hand in pulp noir, fiction that felt like a true crime story, but wasn't quite sure where to start, so the prior night she reached out to her writing community on the CreepyPastarama message board: "What are some true crime tales that are so terrifying that they belong in a horror movie/novel"

Olivia pulled up the site to peruse the replies. Quite a few comments and subsequent conversations had been started in the thread. Plenty of good suggestions but nothing that really jumped out at Olivia. The Toy Box Killer, The Toolbox Killers, Albert Fish, The Night Stalker... all excruciatingly cruel and terrible in their own right but all stories that felt like they'd been tackled or used as inspiration before, many times over. They'd all been done to death. Olivia was moments away from her ADHD switching to a brand-new topic entirely when she noticed a tiny red circle over her inbox icon: a private message.

Oh god, please don't be unsolicited dick pics, "nice guy" outrage, or cringy crush confessions. Please don't be something – worse.

It was a message from a user she had never come across before: LTLblakmajikninja17. Looked like it was a private response to her true crime thread, which gave her pause. Trolls and keyboard cowboys usually saved their worst and most vitriolic comments for private messages. Olivia prepared herself to handle any nonsense that might be lurking behind the link. There was plenty of pent-up emotions to spare if she needed to give a random net nerd a proper dragging through the mud. She took one deep breath for the bullshit and clicked open the message.

LTLblakmajikninja17:
RE:What are some true crime tales that
    are...
Hi.
My name is Larry. I know you don't know
me, but I've read all of your stories. You
are an incredibly talented writer.
    I especially liked the one about the
floating werewolf lady of Mexico. I heard
rumors that it's starting to circulate as
an urban legend and people really think
that stuff is real. That's pretty cool.

(Olivia's story '*Lobavuella*' was *not* about a werewolf. It was a ghost story about a floating woman wearing the flayed skin of a wolf as a mask & it took place in Cuba, not Mexico.)

Anyways, I wanted to tell you about a true crime story that I know. Didn't want to post on the board though because people tend to think I'm crazy or making shit up. Or worse, they think I'm some sort of shill for MalAttack or CarcosaTech. Simple minds don't understand. Not like I know you will, this stuff is right up your alley.

Now this is going to sound fake, because the news story that you've surely heard already is in fact, fake. A cover up. I know this shit is real because it happened to my dad. It happened to my friend from next door too. I told them not to watch it. I'm not responsible for what happened.

The story I'm referring to is the MalAttack Hoax murder/suicide back in 2005. I'm sure you're familiar with it but I have proof that it was NOT a hoax. Before my father met the same fate, he found something terrible. He found the original, undoctored video of the murder. I don't know how it reached his hands, but I have reason to believe that everything that happened to him after finding it was because of that video. He described it in great detail but begged me to never watch so, I never did. When I tried to get rid of the disc it was on, well… curiosity got the best of my neighbor. He wouldn't listen to my warning! Two days later he and his two friends were found with their necks sliced open.

This is the part where you might stop

believing me.

The guy or the thing that did all of this… It's a cybernetic demon. It's a virus with a physical form, well technically it's an antivirus.

We are the virus in his eyes. Actually, it doesn't have eyes. It's complicated.

His/Its name is Render and it's like an overpowered, demonic entity assassin. Pure evil with a switchblade and the face of a monster.

Sorry, I know I suck at writing this. You're so good at it. I thought maybe you could be the one to tell the tale, just like, tell everyone it's fiction like the rest of your stories. Then it can live and die as a creepypasta and nothing more. So, no one else gets hurt.

("a creepypasta and nothing more." That one cut right through her.)

So, if you want to hear the full story, I can tell you everything. I still have the CD (don't ask how I got it back) but I refuse to give it to anyone else. I can show you… other proof though…. If you need it.

Please let me know if you're interested. If not, no worries. I don't blame you.
     -LTL

The end of the email included a few links to news articles about the cases involving the deaths Larry had mentioned. Olivia had to admit; poor grammar, ramblings and all, her curiosity was piqued. She did remember the original hoax story; it was all over the news when she was in high school. She didn't remember anything about a techno-demon manhunter though. Kind of takes the story out of true crime territory once you add in a supernatural villain. Then again, she *loved* a good monster. She wrote back.

StygianStewardess:
RE:RE:What are some true crime tales that are...
    Hi Larry,
    Thank you for the kind words and thank you for being a faithful reader!
    I'm going to be honest, you're right. I don't believe you. However, I am intrigued to hear your unique perspective. What's this "other proof" you speak of? If it's *really* real, you might want to take it to the cops. Not little ol' me.
    Like I said though, I am intrigued, and at the moment, a little desperate to get out of my own head so...
    Show me what you got!
    ~SS

Shit, did that sound mean? she thought to herself immediately after hitting send. *Oh well. This should be fun...* she continued monologuing in her head, *What's one more can of worms?*

The playlist switched to a poppy glitchcore song by GRIMES, a good song that she was a fan of, but the mood called for something less hectic. Olivia skipped to the next track and *Lovely Bloodflow* by BATHS came on. Apparently, her Spotify was in the mood for artists with their names in all caps.

She drifted through her open tabs and landed on an image gallery showcasing liminal spaces, her new favorite time killer. Each picture felt familiar and yet off-putting at the same time; each empty room, hall, or space they depicted just felt a little wrong or impossible. They also felt like places she had visited before but couldn't quite remember, like a discordant dream. They triggered the same uncanny valley feeling she got from witnessing a CGI animated face that she just knew deep inside wasn't moving the way a human face would move. The same feeling she got from that infamous scene in the Japanese horror film 'Kairo,' when a ghostly woman walks out of the shadows in a very disjointed and inhuman way.

She settled on a particularly unnerving image of an empty white room with black carpet. There was one door, and through it she could see what looked like a long hallway. But at the angle it was facing and by how long it seemed, it didn't make sense. The hallway should have been colliding into the outside wall of the room. Who would build something like that? Combined with the eeriness of the current song, it made chills slither across her arms, raising every hair in their path.

Ding.

Another message.

LTLblakmajikninja17:
RE:RE:RE:What are some true crime tales
    that are...
    Wow, didn't expect you to respond so fast. Wasn't sure if you would at all honestly.
    It's ok that you don't believe me, had a feeling you wouldn't. Going to the cops is pointless though, I've tried. Multiple times. The last time they threatened to get me sent to a home. I don't want to end up like Holloway.
    Here's what I can tell you: everything that my dad told me about that original video.
    Here goes nothing.
    So basically, it's this grainy old

webcam video where you see two guys talking to each other via Yahoo messenger or something similar. One of those old instant messaging apps that had the option to video chat and shit.

So these two guys from the famous case, are like, all freaked out because supposedly the AI chatbots that they both programmed just randomly started talking to each other on their own.

It gets kinda nuts in the part before the clip they showed on the news. The first part that nobody has seen.

One of the chatbots uses these command words to like, unlock the other bot's AI somehow. Ancient Latin or some nonsense.

So basically, these two chatbots, they conduct a summoning ritual, right there in the chat log. Of course, anyone reading that, even anyone that watches it up to that point, they think it's ridiculous.

Cue the clip from the news, where you see a few seconds of video, the two of them tripping out and mentioning the anti-virus software— it cuts to black.

Only this video doesn't end there. The screen comes back to life and lo and behold; Render (that's the name of the entity they summoned) he's standing in the doorway and he is TERRIFYING.

Looks like a combination of Max Head-room, Mac Tonight, & Michael Myers. Pure nightmare fuel.

Render steps forward, and straight up murders the first dude, Rendegger. To add to the insanity, at this point in the video everything is glitching and all of their electronics are going haywire. The audio utter madness.

You can see why I thought you'd be better to tell the story. I'm terrible at writing. I'm all show and no tell, or is it the other way around? I just know, I can't give stories a pulse the way that you do.

Now, you probably still don't believe but I can show you my proof. Another video. One that no one else has seen.

Well, no one but the one detective I showed it to who called me a "deranged film student with an overactive imagination and a severe lack of taste." Which is really stupid on his part, I dropped out of high school freshman year.

See I had the original video on a burnt CD back in the day but like I said, never actually watched it myself. I gave it to my neighbor after my dad passed, I wasn't really thinking about it when I did it, I just wanted to get rid of it. I told him he shouldn't watch it but of course, he did. Watched it together with two of his friends and all three of them ended up dead.

The fucked-up part though? I wasn't going to admit this but, whatever. I've already dumped all this other shit on you. I've already admitted everything I could to authorities. What's the difference?

So, after my neighbor died, I snuck into the crime scene once the cops had left. I found 2 things there that I honestly can't believe they never confiscated as evidence; the original burnt CD, & a video file that my neighbor's webcam had recorded during the mayhem.

That video, I did watch.

That is the video I'm attaching here.

Just a warning: the video is blurry and kind of a mess, but it straight up shows the murder, it shows Render. It's hard to make out but it is still pretty fucked up. You've been warned.

Sorry for the giant info dump but I mean, you did kind of ask for it.

Stay safe.

-LTL

📎 Rvideo(1).mp4

📎

"Well, that was… a lot." Olivia sat there for a while, mulling it over in her head. She read the lengthy email a few more times. It did sound like something she would write. It also sounded a bit ridiculous. Why would that happen? *How* could that happen? Who edited the footage of the original video and sent it to the news and why did they work so hard to cover it up? If this thing kills anyone who watches it like *The Ring*, then what happened to whoever that was? Why did Larry attach two files when he only mentioned the one?

A lot of it didn't add up but, maybe that would work in Olivia's favor. She'd have to change the names and characters out of respect for the dead, the way the Coen brothers & Noah Hawley claimed they did in *Fargo*, but the rest she could work with if no one else had ever heard the full story. Olivia could see the villain becoming a horror icon if she did it right.

She had been longing for new horror icons for a while. Hollywood was long overdue for a new rogues' gallery of monsters. We can only take so many remakes.

She looked again at the attached links. What if this was just another augmented reality game that this Larry character was using to lead Olivia on? Why else would he have included the second, oh-so-cryptic file attachment? Did he know how easy it was to tempt her with something so tantalizing? Was this another stalker trying to get her to play some fucked-up game? The thought made her a little upset. Olivia didn't mind playing an ARG as long as they were well crafted, but she did not appreciate being tricked or undermined into playing mind games. She took another minute to process and decided to message him back.

StygianStewardess:
RE:RE:RE:RE:What are some true crime tales that are...
Hello again Larry,
WOW. That is, some story. In fact, it's absolutely wild and still a little bit hard to believe. I'm sorry, I know you've been told that a lot, but I just have to be real with you.
Now, I'd like you to be real with me before we go any further, Larry.
Is this all an elaborate hoax? Are you trying to bait me into another ARG? Because I just really don't have time for it if that's the case. I appreciate your effort to make an immersive experience, but I just really want to write. I don't want to get involved in a series of rabbit holes.
I have not yet watched the video; I'm more concerned about the second file you attached. Is that part of your game? Or a virus? Maybe you are a MalAttack shill after all. I kid but, seriously... please be

real with me here.
~SS

It only took a moment before she received another reply from Larry.
That was fast.

LTLblakmajikninja17:
RE:RE:RE:RE:RE:What are some true crime
tales that are...
What!?
What 2nd attachment??
I only sent 1!
DO. NOT. CLICK. THAT. LINK!
It's fucking Render.
Fuck
I shouldn't have said shit.
Wtf!FUCK!!
A shill? ARG?? The fuck u talking about?
This is bad
Delete everything. I'm so sorry' fUck
this is bad
Goodbye.

Okay. So, it's definitely an ARG, and not even a well scripted one.
Olivia rolled her eyes and went back to Larry's previous email. The poor guy probably spent a lot of time on this thing. Least she could do was give it a glance, she thought.
She clicked the first attachment and played the video.
Well, Larry was right about one thing: the video is a mess.
The image was grainy and extra digitized. It constantly glitched and the lighting had a terrible strobing effect that almost made Olivia feel sick. She could just barely make out three figures standing in the frame. All three looked to be wearing black hoodies and baggy pants. They started to move but then froze in place. The frame glitched even more, almost to

the point that the entire video looked like an old, distorted VHS tape recording. Suddenly, she could make out a fourth character. *This must be Render*, she thought. She could roughly see his hollow eye sockets and missing nose, below that, a long, toothy smile which made her blood run cold. She couldn't deny that part getting to her. Another glitch, and all three of the black hoodies were clutching at their bleeding throats and falling to the floor. More distortion and what looked like Render exited the frame, it was hard to tell. The video ran for another three minutes but it was simply a still frame of the opposite wall shrouded in darkness.

That was it.

"Ugh, that could be so easily faked, though."

Let's just give him what he wants. Moreover, let's get this over with. There has to be at least a few more viable replies to my original thread by now.

Olivia clicked on the second file as she promised herself, *Only this one. If this opens a whole web of riddles and puzzles to solve, we put it to the side and get back to writing.*

"Awe shit!" she yelled out. "It's a fucking virus!"

Her computer began to glitch and window after window opened up on its own. Badly drawn pixel art portraits of Render were on display in each one. Her music began skipping like trying to play an old scratched CD.

Olivia smacked her hand on the desk hard enough to sting then quickly reached for the power button. Before she could shut it down however, everything stopped. She held her hand in the air, finger hovering centimeters above the button.

One window remained in the center of her screen. The music cut out. The open window was a live webcam feed. There, on the other end, was the real Render. Or at least what looked like him, in the flesh or plastic or whatever he was made of. Just sitting there with his freakishly long teeth in a frozen smile, his eyes and nose looked to be ripped from their respective sockets. As if he could just unplug his organs and appendages. His skeletal face juxtaposed beneath his absurdly perfect blonde pompadour hair, made everything feel even more unsettling. Twisting, serpentine knots grew in Olivia's stomach. He sat in silence but moved his head from side to side, as if he could see through those empty eye caverns.

Olivia's brain raced. Her face felt red hot, but her arms and legs felt cold and numbed. Her whole body was overcome with chills, pins and needles trickling over her flesh, crawling like metallic spiders' legs.

A smaller, second window popped up in the corner of Render's window. It was all black. She knew it was her webcam. Luckily, she always kept a Band-Aid over her camera to make sure no one could spy or creep on her.

She felt a wave of relief, followed immediately by waves of anger. This dude had taken his little game way too far.

"Nice mask, LTL," she said mockingly. "Now kindly fuck off and stay the fuck away from my computer. You will be blocked and reported to your good friends, the police. I told you I had no time for games, dude."

Render cocked his head to the side with his egregiously elongated shit-eating grin, then shook his head violently.

The words "T H I S. I S. N o T. A. G a M E." appeared at the bottom of Render's window.

Olivia rolled her eyes. Her fear now replaced with frustration.

"Boy. Stop. I will admit, I'm impressed by the production value of what you're doing. The mask is super terrifying and looks real as hell. I am very unappreciative of you hacking your way onto my computer though, and like I said, you will be reported. In fact, Larry, I'm going to film this for proof."

Olivia reached for her phone. Render tilted his head as if he could see through his window, as if he were watching her in real time. She brought her phone closer and attempted to swipe to her camera; but before she could, a text popped up from an unknown number.

[Unknown: "N O T. L T L."]

"Okay? Now you have my fucking phone num—"

Olivia paused as Render slowly turned onscreen, revealing a crumpled mass of human, slouched against the wall behind him. From what she could make out, the body had shoulder length brown hair and a ratty goatee. The rest of the face was hard to piece together because it was falling apart, covered in gobs of blood and stab wounds. The name "Larry" floated above the head of the corpse in small, white blocky letters as if pinned in mid-air. Render turned back to the screen, his broad, pin-striped suit shoulders blocking the body from view.

Okay, okay. This, this is just really *good production value... right? Either way, you need to call the cops right now, idiot.*

Olivia looked back to her phone and unlocked it as quickly as possible but was once again foiled before she could do anything. Her phone glitched, flashed on and off, flipped her entire home screen upside down, and flashed the dead battery symbol before shutting off.

The fear came flooding back. She was officially freaked the hell out. Throwing the phone behind her and onto her bed, Olivia grabbed the edges of her desk and screamed at the masked marauder on her screen, "WILL YOU STOP!"

Render tilted his head once again like a puppy that didn't understand, then quickly nodded. Olivia was visibly confused. Was he agreeing to stop?

Render glitched, his body splitting into pixelated fragments before disappearing. Olivia saw a fleeting image of the brutalized body against the wall before the video feed cut to black.

"What the hell was that?" Olivia whispered to the walls. She rested her head in her right hand and rubbed her temple. "Should have just stayed at Coffee Stop, for fuck's sake..." When she gazed up at the corner of her room it suddenly felt much bigger and emptier. She now noticed exactly how alone and vulnerable she was, sitting with a looming sense of dread.

The window that Render had appeared in was left suspended in the middle of her screen. After about a minute, the video feed returned, only now it was an entirely different camera.

"What now?" Olivia groaned.

It was the live feed to an indoor security camera, perched high in the corner of a large bedroom. A woman looked to be sleeping in the bed. Her face was grainy and hard to see, but somehow, she felt awfully familiar to Olivia. The time stamp running in the bottom right corner of the window read: 05:35:16 PM.

Who goes to sleep at 5:30?

Olivia noted the wine glass and pill bottle on the nightstand and put two and two together.

"Well, that's a little sad but, understandable..." Olivia watched the scene for a moment, nervous; she wasn't into voyeurism and was quite sure it's illegal to hack into someone else's webcam. "Why are you showing me this? Is this collateral for you or something?" She wasn't even sure that Render, or whoever the culprit was, could hear her.

Grabbing her mouse, she quickly tried to close the window, but the pointer wouldn't budge. She shook the mouse harder and slammed it down on her table.

"Come on!"

Abruptly, the mirrored closet door next to the sleeping woman's bed slid open on its own. It remained open and eerily still for a few seconds until something emerged from in between the hanging clothes. Olivia already knew what was coming. One black leather glove attached to a black pinstriped suit sleeve poked its way out first and slowly pulled forth Render in all his well-tailored and unsettling horror.

Render looked up, directly into the security camera, and placed one outstretched leather finger in front of his tooth-filled mouth.

"Are you shushing me? Hell no. Can you hear me? Can *she* hear me? Hey lady! Wake up!"

Olivia grabbed her computer and shook it, her clammy hands leaving a trail of moisture on the screen. As her pulse quickened, she did her best to reinforce that this was all just a show. Then again, what if it wasn't?

She yelled out once more, "Wake. Up!"

It was no use. Render shrugged his shoulders awkwardly, one after the other, then looked down at the woman slumbering in her bed. He reached into his breast pocket and pulled out the long, slender handle of his switchblade and staggered forward. He took high, rigid steps, as though he was trying to step over large invisible hurdles. The way he moved reminded Olivia of an old, low budget cartoon, where the frames never really matched up smoothly. Render reached the edge of the bed and leaned over the motionless body. He looked up at the camera one more time, taunting his audience of one.

Olivia sat back and crossed her arms, refusing to give in.

"This is obviously pre-recorded. This is just a stupid game. Stupid, stupid game!" She repeated trying to convince herself. She wanted to just turn off her laptop but, she couldn't stop watching.

Render lifted his right arm into the air, twirling the switch-blade handle between his fingers until it was upside down and pointing directly at the head of the unsuspecting sleeping beauty. Olivia could see his chest moving, whoever was under that mask must be breathing heavily, she thought. She watched as his thumb moved over the switchblade's release trigger and – BAM!

The blade popped out so fast Olivia thought it was another glitch. The thin silver blade jammed into the side of the woman's skull. Her eyes and mouth flew wide open, but she didn't move. Blood pooled around the base of the knife and created a drizzling waterfall down her face. There was so much blood so fast. Olivia felt a lump rise in her throat. The blood kept coming. It poured out of the woman's mouth and onto her pillow, rapidly spreading into a vermillion, cloud-shaped stain. Olivia wanted to barf.

This is all staged, she reminded herself.

Render pulled out the blade and wiped the blood off with his gloved fingers. He began vibrating and shaking his entire body, emitting an electronic buzz that sounded like a swarm of cicadas. Olivia suddenly realized she could actually hear the sound from the video feed and that the soft crackling fuzz she had been hearing for the past three minutes wasn't just her tinnitus. It was the background audio from the webcam.

Render stopped shaking and turned back to the camera one last time. He wiggled his fingers as he waved and then completely blinked out of existence. Render was gone, and Olivia was left with the image of this poor wine-soaked woman bleeding out in her own bed.

Olivia felt dizzy and sick. She struggled with what to believe. It all looked so real. It all *felt* so real. She couldn't even explain why. It just *felt* like something was terribly, terribly wrong, augmented reality game or not. Still, it had to be prefabricated right? People don't just disappear or glitch like that in real life. It had to be special effects. Didn't it?

The background white noise from the camera feed rose and fell. The slain lady in bed let out a soft gurgle. Olivia shook the mouse again but to no avail.

What she heard next in the live stream made her heart do a triple backflip into the pit of her guts.

Footsteps, coming from the hallway just outside the bedroom door. Small, child-sized footsteps.

"Mom?"

"Nope. No, no, no!" she shouted. Olivia knew that voice.

The shadow reached the doorway first, followed by a young boy, wearing large headphones and holding a tablet in his hands. He was still looking down at his game, not even aware of what he was walking into.

"Mom! Wake up!" he shouted before he finally looked up and saw the gruesome scene before him.

Olivia saw his eyes and confirmed all her suspicions at once: the murdered mother on the mattress was Chrysanthemum, the coffee snob from earlier that day, and her creepy, possibly psychic, son had just wandered into the most horrific thing that he may ever witness.

Olivia screamed. She jumped up and slammed her laptop shut. She slapped a hand over her mouth and stumbled backwards to her bed. She crawled on top of it and backed all the way up to the wall, grabbing a pillow and clutching it close to her chest. Her mouth filled with saliva and her head felt like it was swelling, her skin tightening. She fought back the urge to vomit, put her face into the pillow and screamed again.

Render was real. She was now witness to an actual murder and some way, somehow, this phantasmagorical entity was targeting her.

Olivia's head spun in circles that felt more like Möbius strips. The room whirled around her as she became light-headed and faint.

She closed her eyes and passed out.

FOUR

OLIVIA'S BRAIN FELT LIKE A hot air balloon when she woke up in a daze a few hours later. She tried to recall everything clearly, but it felt like a distant nightmare.

Please God, tell me that was all a dream.

As she regained her wherewithal, her mind raced between images of Render, Chrysanthemum and her son, and her marijuana induced hallucination of her brother and everything he had said. She crawled slowly out of her covers and sat on the edge of her bed, where she sobbed quietly. She looked at her phone, which was no longer dead, glitching, or upside down. She thought about calling the police but, what if she *was* just going crazy? She started to call Taylor but hung up before it rang once. She clutched her pillow and stared at the wall. She could hear the blood rushing through her ears, tiny crimson waves rolling around in her head.

The day seemed so promising that morning. Olivia loved stormy fall days. She had smelled the dry leaves and the petrichor from the damp asphalt as soon as she left her house.

The smell of roasting coffee at Coffee Stop had been just a hint more robust and luscious. The old yellow-paged book she had brought to read on her breaks had even more of that old library smell that would waft up to her nose when she fanned the pages. Those early hours promised her all the luxuries of a warm autumn breeze but all they delivered was a bitter chill and harsh unrelenting showers of tension.

She rattled off the list of events in her head like she was flipping through a rolodex of anxiety.

She still wasn't quite sure what to make of it. When she tried to look at it from an outside perspective it felt so stupid. It felt like she was really, literally losing her mind.

All the while, she kept staring at the empty void of space on her bedroom wall. The gap that used to be covered in a collage of magazine clippings, old concert tickets, and candid Kodak moments. Olivia had devoted cumulative days of her life to that collage but after her family passed, she couldn't look at it anymore without crying. Each piece was carefully taken down and stored in a shoebox under her bed and the spot was cleared. That spot could have started smoking if she had stared any longer, but she turned and looked at the clock on her night-stand. It was 7:30 and she still hadn't eaten.

Pizza. Pizza and a movie are all I've ever needed.

Olivia made the call and browsed for something to watch while she waited for her cheese and meat-covered security blanket to arrive.

Three episodes of *The Office*, one stoner comedy flick, and half of a pepperoni, sausage, and jalapeno pizza later, Olivia was starting to feel like herself again. She even laughed out loud when she thought about what an insane fever dream the entire day had been. Laughter that was quickly stifled by the overwhelming fear that she still may or may not be an accomplice to murder.

She decided to text Taylor about it: "Hey Taytay, um, I have something real weird-ish to tell you. I don't even know where to start."

Before Olivia could finish typing the next message Taylor was calling. Just seeing her name on the caller ID was a relief. She knew Taylor would drop anything she was doing if she thought that Olly needed her.

They talked for well over an hour. Olivia told her everything as best she could remember. They discussed whether or not she was at risk, being hacked, being stalked, or being baited into an elaborate game like Olivia had originally postulated.

"Olly. Do you remember the time you ate, like, three weed cookies in one sitting before going to see my little sister's ballet recital?"

"Oh. My. God. The Wildwood cave goblin incident."

"Yeah…"

"Okay, no. You only had *one* pot cookie, and you even admitted to seeing some wild shit too. Those cookies had absolutely no business being that potent."

"They were quadruple strength, Olly."

"Nobody told me!"

The duo laughed for a good minute.

"*Dude*," Olivia wiped the happy tears out of her eyes, " I legit thought your sister and her dance troop were all tiny cave goblins and they wanted to take my soul."

Taylor screamed laugher on the other end of the phone.

"They all kept staring at me!"

Taylor regained her breath and tried to talk through her giggle fits. "Uh yeah, of course they were. You looked like a crack head, and you were literally clawing into the arms of your chair, breathing through your teeth all hard." Taylor mimicked the intense breathing and burst out laughing again. "Okay, okay," she said in between breaths, "but do you remember how even after you came down from that high, you still *reallly* believed that what you saw was real?"

Olivia stopped laughing and got quiet.

"I know you only smoked like one half of a measly joint but I mean…" Taylor took her time to tread as carefully as she could around the subject. "Combined with everything else that's happened to you this last year, and you even said, you know that vision of Alejandro wasn't real. Maybe…"

Olivia stayed quiet for another beat. She thought hard about what Taylor was implying. She was probably right but, what did that mean about Olivia's psyche?

"No, yeah, you're—You're probably right. Gotta be honest though, sis, I'm still a little freaked out," Olivia shyly admitted.

"You? Olivia Peramo? The Cuban queen of all things creepy, disturbing, and terrifying? The self-proclaimed stewardess and my personal sherpa into the stygian abyss of what we fear most, afraid of a stalker slash hacker with wayyyy too much time on their hands?" Taylor paused and waited for a reaction. Olivia gave none; she only held her breath. Taylor could tell something was different this time. "Oh, hon."

"I'm okay. You're right. I know you are." Olivia laughed nervously. "If it's real though, I just—"

"*If* it's real, well, we'll just have to figure out the next steps. Together. Michael is a lawyer, so we can go over exactly what happened and make sure you're not, like, complicit or whatever."

"I don't think I'm an accessory, Tay, but isn't it illegal to witness a crime and not report it?"

"I honestly don't know. Do you want me to ask Mike?"

"No!" Olivia shouted louder than she meant to. "No, please don't say anthing, to anyone yet."

"Okay, okay, don't trip. Like we said, it's probably all just a messed up game or the beautifully maniacal inner workings of Olivia Peramo's head."

Olivia smiled and shook her head. "You're stupid."

"You're smelly," Taylor shot back.

"Hey! Don't call me smelly!" said Olivia, faking an angry voice.

"Well, then don't smell."

Even when they were having a go at each other and digging up old inside jokes, Taylor always knew how to put a smile on Olivia's face and wash away the wake of misery vultures that perpetually circled overhead.

"K-k Taytay… I think I'm gonna get some shut eye and try to get enough rest so I'm not a complete wreck tomorrow night. Just a small one."

"Ooh! Somebody remembered on their own!"

Olivia laughed, "Shut up."

"Oh!" Taylor interjected, "Bring your laptop maybe? Some of Michael's buddies from high school are coming, and they are like massive tech nerds. They all work at that big ass computer store over in St. Charles. You don't have to tell them what happened; just say that you think you might have been hacked and see if they can make sure you're clean?"

"Eh, don't really feel like a tech desk meeting in the middle of your engagement party is ideal party etiquette, my love."

"Hmm. Yeah, you right," said Taylor. "Well, at least you can bring it up or mingle with them and see if you can bring your lappytoppy over to their store on Monday. Who knows, maybe you'll fall for one of them 'cause you're totally a nerd too!"

"Please don't set me up."

"I'm *kidding*… besides, we have… someone else we want you to meet."

"Please don't, Taylor."

"He's really *cute*."

"Taylor!"

"I love you. See you tomorrow, *byyyyye!*" Taylor said so quickly it almost sounded like one long word.

"Don't!"

click

Taylor ended the call before Olivia could slip in another word of protest.

"Bitch." Olivia said out loud with a smile on her face.

She took one last glance at her phone, then her laptop. She thought about browsing both to make sure that there were no other signs of Render or Larry. She decided that some things are better left for morning and kept away from her devices. She turned on the television in her room and played another episode of *The Office*. The TV was her adult night light and *The Office* was her favorite lullaby. Olivia drifted off to sleep in minutes.

FIVE

A FAINT ELECTRIC CRACKLE SNAPPED through the air just above her face.

Olivia rubbed the sleep out of her eyes. The room was foggy and grey. Rubbing her eyes once more, the room came into focus.

The walls were bright white. Her LED lights and old concert posters were gone. No flatscreen on the wall. This was not Olivia's room. She sat up straight on the bed, trying to gain her bearings. The bed she was in felt alien. Small white mattress, thin white sheets, no pillows at all, and an alabaster white bedframe. Olivia quickly took her hands off the bed as though it was hot to the touch. She wrapped her arms around herself and assessed the rest of the room.

The walls and ceiling were a stark, blank white. An empty void. There were two white doors, one on either side of the room and nothing else. The only thing that stood out was the dark grey, almost black carpet. The coarse, needle-punched textile spanned the entire floor and looked like something you would find in an office supply store.

Olivia's breathing became rapid as she ran her hand through her long dark hair. She knew this room, but she didn't. It felt like she was in the midst of an urban alien abduction. Kidnapped in the backroom of an Ikea perhaps? It was genuinely disorienting. She stood up and her legs almost gave, but she steadied herself and regulated her breathing.

Olivia checked herself. She was still wearing her oversized Wu-Tang sleep shirt that she had worn to bed. There were no signs of anyone touching her that she could see. A slight sense of relief came over her, but she was still tense and ready to hit fight or flight mode at any second.

As she took a step toward the doorway to the right of the bed, it suddenly dawned on her. This was the same room she had been fixated on earlier last night while browsing liminal spaces. Or if it wasn't, someone had done a damned good job of replicating it. The hairs on the back of her neck stood up as she thought about the implication.

The sound of static rippled through the space around her. Olivia clenched her fists until her knuckles turned white.

Something was coming.

The door she was walking toward slowly creaked inward on it's own.

She was expecting to see her new friend on the other side, but when it swung all the way open, it only revealed the same blank, crooked hallway from the image she had seen on her computer.

"Okay. This has to be a dream. We're dreaming. Wake up, Olly. Wake the fuck up, Olivia!"

She shook her head as she yelled at herself. She tried pinching her cheek. Nothing worked. Dream or not, she wasn't getting out of this yet.

The static buzz grew louder and moved down the hall. It beckoned her. Something was at the other end of that hallway, waiting for her. The noise became a throaty, metallic, gutteral moan. The voice cried out in dial-tone. She knew that it wanted her, and she couldn't stop herself from moving forward.

As Olivia crept around the corner and entered the impossibly angled hall, she looked down the long white tunnel and saw exactly who she thought she'd see, standing dead center in the middle of the corridor.

Render stood completely still, only mere feet away from Olivia. He suddenly lifted a gloved hand and waved hello. His shiny black shoes glinted in the light. His perfectly pressed and pin-striped suit looked too crisp to be real. The black leather gloves, spotless. His blonde quaffed hair, too pretty for such a hideous monster. Those long stretched out teeth, as white as the walls surrounding them. That never-ending, blood-curdling smile. The bloody skeletal sockets where the eyes and nose once lived.

Seeing his face this close up made her stomach turn.

She braced herself and assumed a guarded stance. She waited for him to attack.

Nothing happened.

Render put his hand down and stared with his hollow eyes.

"What the hell do you want from me?" Olivia demanded.

Render said nothing. He ticked his head to the left and cracked his neck, turned, and began to walk towards the other end of the hallway. Every step that he took, his body shook violently, emitting grinding clicks and clacks with each movement. As he got closer the smell of burning wires filled the room.

Olivia kept her guard up and watched as he ambled to the only other door at the far end of the hall. The door next to her slammed shut, causing her to jump. She reached out as fast as she could to try and open the door again but it was locked and wouldn't budge.

When she turned to see Render again, he was opening the door in front of him and exiting the hall.

"Oh hell no. You are not locking me in this long-ass hallway!"

Olivia choked down her trepidation and sprinted toward the opposite end of the hall. The hall stretched as she ran.

Olivia kept running and running for what felt like an eternity. Render stood in the doorway until she finally inched closer. Then he turned to leave. She got to the door just before it shut behind Render. She grabbed the doorknob as hard as she could, yanking it backwards with all her might. The door flew open. Olivia jumped into the room like the walls were collapsing behind her. The door slammed shut.

Render was nowhere to be found.

Somehow, she was back in the same white room that she had woken up in.

"What. The. Fuck," Olivia panted.

As she regained her train of thought, the incessant buzzing returning. It rose from the door behind her.

How is that coming from behind me?

How am I back in this infernal room?

Why can't I wake up? she screamed inside her mind.

The door swung open again.

Render emerged, towering over her. For the first time, he spoke.

"What's wrong, *mija*?"

It was her father's voice, but it was robotic and raspy. It was wrong. All wrong.

Render grabbed Olivia by the shoulders and shook his head furiously in every direction.

"You have so many bugs and threats in your life, Olivia. This is why you summoned me." He continued to mimic her father's sweet voice with his thick Cuban accent—if it was only smashed into a food proccessor and thrown at the back of a metallic fan.

It was beginning to piss Olivia off.

"I can help you," Render's entire body was now vibrating and convulsing. "Let me clear it all away for you, *Muñequita*."

Muñequita. Spanish for baby doll. Only her father ever called her by that name, and only her father was allowed to.

"How fucking dare you!" she screamed and shoved Render as hard she could.

Render flew backwards, but he seized Olivia's hand and pulled her down with him.

The floor was gone.

They fell into an infinite void.

Olivia felt her stomach dropping as she plummeted.

She heard her father's voice again, his real voice this time. It gently whispered in her ear.

"Wake up, Olivia. Please wake up, my darling. You do not need to hold on to all this darkness. You can let go of all these strings and attachments you have."

Olivia felt lighter with every word he spoke. Fragments of her guilt and anguish broke away from her and crystalized in the air.

"No matter what happens, Mija, we love you."

She tried to reply, *"What's going to happen?"* but nothing came out.

She continued to fall. She felt like she might be falling forever.

Down,

down,

down into the nothing

until,

THUD.

Olivia crashed into the floor of her own bedroom.

SIX

FIERY, AMBER TINTED LEAVES KISSED the edges of the
murky green pond in Olivia's backyard. Autumn in Missouri had a way of setting the foliage ablaze and decorating itself
for the holidays. It was always Olivia's favorite time of the year.
She sat at the clear beveled table on her patio, staring out at the
cozy morning scenery. It was calm and quiet, save for a small
family of ducks, no doubt commenting on the beautiful foliage
amongst themselves.

The pond was small, roughly the size of a baseball diamond,
and it was the only thing that separated the Peramo's backyard from a modestly sized forest. Those woods used to haunt
Olivia as a child. She would stare across the water and deep
into the trees, wondering what was staring back at her. She
loved exploring them, even if her parents would only let her go
if her brother came along to supervise. Alejandro never wanted
to, but he had a hard time saying no to his sister. Ally used to
joke that his friends would never let him hear the end of it, if
they knew what a big wuss he was and that his little sister was

braver than him and that he needed her to make him feel safe in the deep, dark woods.

"Pssh! Yeah, right," she'd say. "Remember the time we went to the Lake of the Ozarks, and I almost got bit by that nasty copperhead? You swooped like a frickin' superhero and flattened that thing with your Eastwood. *Wabam!*" Olivia imitated her brother crushing the snake's skull. "Kinda stupid though; you could have died if you missed."

"Shhh. Shut up, *enana*! It's also kinda *illegal* to kill a snake in Missouri so don't go tellin' people about that, okay?"

They needed each other just the same. Olivia was a brave little *chica* on her own but alongside Alejandro, she felt invincible, and vice versa. They protected each other through thick and thin. Olivia remembered walking to the edge of the forest and looking back at her house. Sometimes, she felt like *she* was the who or what that was looking back at herself from across the way. Glitching in time and watching herself through a warped mirror.

Olivia pulled her gaze away and looked down at the large, tightly rolled joint on the table in front of her.

To smoke, or not to smoke?

It *was* perfect weather, and it *would* pair so splendidly with the homemade café latte that was currently warming her hands, but what if it really was the cause for all the chaos that was yesterday?

Olivia had spent the early hours of the morning checking her computer, along with every other electronic in the house. No sign of hackers, no sign of Render. She watched the morning news and checked every news site; so far, no reports of a local woman found murdered in her bed. It all seemed like a bad trip. A terrible, rotten, mindfuck of a bad trip.

If she was being honest though, she had come down from worse trips than that. Magic mushrooms had done a number on her back in high school.

Yesterday was wrought with stress and my anxiety getting the best of me... Today, I feel perfectly at peace. C'mon, Olly, this is not *our first rodeo.*

She placed her mug on the table and grabbed the joint and her lighter. After lighting it and taking her first inhale, she scrolled through her phone for a good song to set the vibe. After a minute or two and three more puffs, she landed on "Black Magic Woman," the original by Fleetwood Mac. It reminded her of both her parents in a comforting way.

Her mother, because Fleetwood Mac was her all-time favorite band. You couldn't get through a single song on *Rumours* without Mama singing every word off-key. Her papa, because the song itself made her think of how he would *always* insist that "Santana did it better." He would fight tooth and nail to defend Carlos Santana.

We were quite the musical family, for a family of people completely devoid of musical talent.

Olivia watched the smoke swirl out of her lips and cast a thin grey veil over the imagery in front of her. She tilted her head back and looked up at the awning that covered the back porch, curving against the silver sky. She thought about what it was like to move to this house when she was so little. She didn't remember much at all about Miami, where she was born; she just remembered walking up to this massive house of stone and bricks, surrounded by an enchanted forest for the first time. She thought it was a castle back then.

When her father had landed a big-time job in Missouri, he originally wanted to move to a town named Cuba. He always wanted to go back to where he was from, in any way that he could.

Shame he never really got to...

When they finally arrived in the Midwest, however, they found out how vastly different the small town of Cuba, Missouri was compared to Carlos Peramo's home country. Plus, it was too far of a commute from his new job. Not to mention with the perks of his new gig, they could afford much nicer digs than what Cuba, MO had to offer. So, they settled here in Wildwood. In El Castillo de Peramo.

It was a wonderland to Ally and Olly during their childhood. Though the house became modernized, as did the furniture and her mother's decorating style over the years, it always had a bit of that 90s design flair to it, at least on the inside. Olivia loved that about the home. Like every 90s kid that didn't have a terrible upbringing, the 90s was her favorite era. The music, the movies, the cartoons and TV shows; sometimes she even yearned for the cheesy classic commercials from those days. It was where she found herself and when she fell in love with horror. *Ghostbusters, Goosebumps,* and *Are You Afraid of the Dark* had her hooked at a young age.

Thin veils of mist descended from the clouds and a faint, gentle breeze ruffled the tops of the thick forest's trees. Olivia squinted into the distance; she could have sworn she heard the far-off buzz of cicada.

That's fucking weird. Why would cicada be out at this time of year and in this type of weather?

Perhaps the distant hum of a far-off telephone pole? She wondered, but the closest power line was miles away and she'd certainly never heard one here before.

The song playing on her phone skipped and repeated the line, *"Turning my heart into stone."* But Olivia was so focused on the strange atmospheric noise that she didn't notice. The noise faded as the rain started coming down a little harder, and she relaxed into her chair once again, taking a long sip from her creamy vanilla roast. Raindrops hitting the lake, on an autumn day with a lovely joint and the perfect cup of coffee triggered a deep sense of stillness inside her. As much as she longed for her halcyon days, moments like this brought her unbridled serenity. She could almost feel her missing family members sitting in the empty seats around the table with her.

Olivia's tranquil reminiscence was cut short when her stomach rudely interrupted with an audible gurgle.

She grinned like a child at the realization that cold pizza was waiting for her in the kitchen. She put out the joint and bounded inside to grab her snack.

The TV in the living room was still on the local news. Olivia inactively watched as she gorged her cold pizza slices. The weather report showed that the current storm would let up by tonight and the rest of the week was due for a little partly cloudy sunshine and warmer temperatures. A fluff piece about a local bakery was next up but was immediately cut for breaking news.

A blonde reporter stood outside a home in St. Charles, roped off by caution tape and swarming with police. Olivia read the chyron twice as it didn't quite sink in the first time.

"LIVE: ST. CHARLES MOTHER FOUND STABBED TO DEATH IN HER OWN BED"

Olivia's ears rang, drowning out the sound of the news reporter's voice. She dropped her pizza and ran to the couch to grab the remote. She shut off the TV and sat in silence. She stared into her tinted reflection in the blank screen, blurred and out of focus. For a second, Olivia couldn't see her eyes, just black hollows and skeletal features over her own face.

Fuck.

SEVEN

"OKAY, BUT, YOU WERE HIGH again right?" Taylor asked in hushed tones as she handed Olivia a beer.

Olivia had packed up everything she needed, gotten dressed as fast as possible, and booked it to Taylor's house early that afternoon. Taylor was beyond giddy to see her when she opened the door. She had been scared that Olivia would bail last minute. Olivia carried quite the flaky history with Taylor, but when she did show up, she always showed up early, hours before the party, so they could have some QHT (quality home-girl time) and help with whatever was needed to prepare for the party.

Taylor had not expected to see Olivia so out of sorts, however. She knew something was wrong the second she opened the door and saw the look in Olivia's big brown eyes. She quickly ushered Olivia inside and offered refreshments while she got ready. After she dressed, they continued their QHT on the balcony attached to Taylor's master bedroom.

"Ugh. Yeah, I was high, but this is real Taylor. Look it up.

It's all over Fox 2. Every news channel probably," Olivia said as quietly as possible. Michael was still getting ready just inside the room, and as privy as he was to pretty much everything that happened in either of the girls' lives, Olivia was still embarrased and didn't want to involve anyone else in her manic mess just yet.

"I know, I uh—I saw it before you came over," admitted Taylor, watching over her shoulder as her fiancee finally finished and left the room to make more preparations downstairs. "Love you, babe!" she called out as he exited. She turned back to face Olivia and took another swig of her beer. "There's no way that they could trace the camera thing back to you, though, right?"

Olivia gulped down half her drink and stared out into the cloud of lightning bugs that gathered beneath the trees as the sun slowly crept beneath the horizon. For a fleeting moment she thought about how strange it was to see them in the Fall, but it had been quite the muggy Autumn already and everything that had seen as of late had been beyond strange as it were. "I don't know, dude. That's what I'm so damn scared about. This isn't a silly game anymore and I don't even know how to fucking stop it. Or why it's targeting me."

Taylor rested her chin on her glass bottle and processed everything Olivia was telling her. "Why *is* it targeting you? You said that he killed everyone in the videos you saw, right?"

"Yeah."

"But so far, he's only showed himself to you through webcams and… Zoom calls?"

"I don't know if it was Zoom, but, yeah."

"Maybe he's trying to, like, fuck with you or intimidate you before he comes after you?"

Olivia turned to her best friend with wide eyes and finished her beer in another gulp.

"Well, that's really reassuring."

"Sorry! I'm just trying to figure it out. You're scaring me, Olly. Why did that loser asshole have to send you anything in the first place?"

"Right?" Olivia put her empty bottle down and pulled her legs onto the chair, hugging her knees in front of her face. "It's like, a 'World of His Own,' but—"

"A world of what?"

"'A World of His Own.' It's an old episode of *The Twilight Zone*, where the characters that this writer creates come to life and start interacting with him. Even his wife finds out she's one of his creations. It's one of the more comedic episodes, but it used to be one of my favorites. Now, I feel like I've written so many cheesy, scary stories that they're all happening to me for real. Only, I never even got the chance to write this one down."

"Girl, you really smoke too much weed."

They both burst out laughing, and Olivia shoved Taylor playfully. "It's not the weed, stupid."

"I know, I know, but *why* is this happening to you, though!? Let me message this monster-man. I need to tell him to leave my Smelly the F alone!"

"You know, last night I had this backwards-ass dream about him… And, he said something like, I asked for this to happen or this is what I wanted or some shit," said Olivia, getting lost in the lightning bugs again.

"I mean, you only asked for true crime-inspired stories on a message board, I wouldn't say that was directly asking for it. Plus, that was *your* dream, so that's just *your* subconscious trying to guilt trip you."

"Yeah…" Olivia stalled. "Well, there was this one, uh, summoning circle tweet that I put out yesterday morning…"

"A tweet? Like with the tiny candle emojis and a prayer in the middle?" barked Taylor.

"Yeah but—"

"Olly! You really think you actually summoned a serial killer with a bad meme using emojis in a circle on Twitter?"

"Bitch! It's a synthetic, freaking cyber-demon thing! I don't know how this shit works!!"

The girls cracked up; it was all so insane at this point.

Olivia finally calmed down and looked at her best friend.

Taylor was especially done up for her engagement party. She looked stunning. Overwhelming guilt crashed into Olivia's chest. Once again, she was burdening her friend on a night that was supposed to be about her.

"Ugh. I'm so sorry. Let's just try and forget about it tonight. This night is for you and Michael. Please don't worry about my bullshit." Olivia offered an apologetic puppy dog face.

"Homegirl, don't trip. You are basically my sister. I'm here no matter what. Whether I am Taylor Trudeau —"

"True tho!"

"Or Taylor Baeler —"

"Eww don't remind me that your new name is going to rhyme!"

"I will always be here to sort out the chaos in your crazy little skull, asshole."

Olivia jumped out of her seat and gave Taylor a skeleton crushing hug.

"Love you, Taytay."

"Love you, Olly."

"C'mon, lets go show off this new rock muffugga!" Taylor sang as she wiggled her ring finger and skipped back into her room.

Guests started trickling in around eight. Olivia did her best to tag along with Taylor, but at a certain point she felt like a needy puppy. She waited until Taylor was deep into a boring conversation with her soon-to-be in-laws and slowly dissolved her presence from the room.

Olivia wandered the sprawling skeleton of the home while trying to ignore the song "Here" by Alessia Cara that was playing over the speakers throughout the house. Not that Olivia didn't like the song — it was actually one of her favorites — but at the moment she felt it was a little too on the nose to play the aloof, disenchanted character in the background of the party during a song about the exact same thing. Half-stepping and heel-turning her way through crowded corridors, she kept her eyes on the floor and danced around unwanted, awkward conversations. The last thing Olivia wanted to do right now was get caught up in a "Oh my god, how have you been?" or a, "What have you been up to?" or even a, "So, what do you do for work?" It was like being at a highschool party again. Only now, everyone was pretending to be grown up with fancy jobs, fancy clothes, and fancy cars. Olivia probably had more money in the bank than any of them, but she had no reason to flaunt it and no desire to discuss the details of how that came to be. Ducking and dodging the red plastic cups full of cheap beer and people shouting at each other to be heard over the music, Olivia slipped into the kitchen to grab a beer for herself.

To her surprise, the kitchen was a nice change of pace. At most highschool parties back in the day, the kitchen was a social hot spot. Tonight, the music was quieter and there was only a small group of five huddled around the kitchen table who were so engaged in their own conversation that they hardly noticed Olivia until the refrigerator door slammed shut a little louder than she intended. All five of the heads whipped around to look at Olivia, a deer in headlights holding a green glass bottle.

"Sorry. Door is so dang heavy," Olivia said awkwardly with an accusatory thumb over her shoulder.

So dang heavy? Seriously Olivia? She cringed on the inside.

The one female at the table piped up first.

"You're good. That thing has been slamming shut all night. I think we just got caught off guard this time because we were all so enthralled in Jason's speech here," Theresa said sarcastically as she motioned to the dark-haired, olive-skinned man seated in the middle. He gave a small salute and a wink as she continued: "He's been pontificating all night about his 'no knock out rule' in Dungeons and Dragons." The large red haired man at the opposite table let out a groan and swigged his drink.

Olivia wasn't quite sure how to respond. "Oh, um, right."

"I'm sorry." The girl at the table laughed. "We — uh, tend to get a bit uber-nerdy after a couple of these," she said, tapping her finger on the side of her bottle. "I'm Theresa. This fellow on my left is Percy. The gentle giant with the fiery beard over there is Hector, and of course I've already inadvertently introduced Jason, here."

"We are — the Greek Squad!" said Jason with a flourish.

"Like the Geek Squad but with a little 'r' in parantheses, 'cause we're all pretty big into Greek mythology and whatnot," chimed in Percy.

Hector groaned again. "Can we please try to not to be so uncool right off the bat when meeting real people in the real world? For once? Hi, by the way."

Olivia laughed. They all seemed harmless and definitely more her speed than the rest of the high-faluten guests surrounding them. She leaned against the counter and engaged the G(r)eek Squad.

"Hi. I'm Olivia, and, you're totally fine. I love Greek mythology — I reference it a lot for, like, story telling and shit."

"Writer?" asked Jason.

"Uh, yeah, kind of. Mainly, like, creepypastas and stuff. More like a blogger if I'm being honest." Olivia laughed sheepishly.

"I *love* a good creepy story," said Theresa. "Don't sell youself short though, I've read some creepypastas online that are honestly better written than some horror novels. Sometimes, the really good ones even get big-ass movie deals. I'd say it is one-hundred percent valid to consider yourself a writer."

Olivia liked Theresa already.

"Well, thank you."

"So, how do you know Michael and Taylor?"

"Oh, Taylor has been my best friend since the fifth grade."

"Ah, the maid of honor then, I'm sure," said Theresa. "We all went to high school with Michael. He used to be our DM, er, dungeon master… kind of like the leader for all the table top games we used to play."

"We *still* play," insisted Jason. "Some people just believe they're too cool to have fun these days. I have taken up the mantle of DM and I'd venture so far as to say the campaigns we play now have never been better."

Hector snorted and almost spit up his beer. "Get over yourself, dude. We're not in game. You can drop the *Lord of the Manor* act." He turned to Olivia. "So what do you do for work?"

Damnit.

"Well, besides writing, um, I am a barista. At Coffee Stop." She couldn't decide whether it was worse to lie about her job or tell the truth.

"Right on," replied Hector. "We're all clerks too. Well I guess, technically, I own the shop now so, a bit higher than a clerk at this point, but it still feels like I'm a damn cashier." They all laughed except Jason. "It's my dad's electronic shop. Fred's Electronics over in St. Louis. I inherited the place from him when he passed and hired this ragtag hive of scum and villainy to run the shop with me."

"Nice Star Wars reference," said Olivia. Theresa started beaming to see that Olivia was at least a bit of a nerd herself.

"I'm double the clerk." Theresa laughed. "When I'm not schlepping around with these heathens at Fred's, I also do stock work at the Schnuk's in Wildwood."

"Oh, my God, I'm like literally around the corner from there! That's cool. It's oddly comforting to meet fellow clerks that are actual adults, not to mention locals."

"We're not all clerks," said Jason, sounding quite annoyed. "I am an assistant manager, thank you very much."

"Ah, so he's the Dwight," said Olivia, and the table around Jason erupted in laughter.

"And who are you? Wednesday Addams?" Jason shot back.

"Psssh... More like Morticia Addams in that black dress," said Theresa admiringly. Olivia blushed.

Percy turned around in his chair to check Olivia out. He snapped in agreement. "Mmm-hmm. A fine-ass hispanic Morticia Addams with the matching leather jacket. Like, *dayumn!*" He turned in his seat and looked back at Jason. "And you over here lookin like an emaciated Lurch, tryin to talk?" The group of friends burst into laughter again. Everyone except Jason. Jason was not so easily amused.

"Excuse me," he said with a sour face, getting up and wandering off into the party.

"Seat just opened up," said Hector, kicking out Jason's vacant seat from beneath the table. "Care to join us?"

Olivia was happy to.

They spent the next few hours drinking and discussing everything from old horror flicks to Star Wars and even a little bit of the basics about Dungeons and Dragons. Olivia was finally feeling a little buzzed and slightly more open to deeper discussions. Still, she had enough wits about her to keep her comments vague and veiled.

"Okay so, if I were to make a DnD character, what kind of spell would I cast to summon another being?"

"Well, it depends what class you pick and, more specifically, what kind of 'being' you're attempting to summon," replied Hector.

Percy took a break from zoning out into his phone and spoke up: "Almost every class can summon certain things at a certain point. For instance, I'm a tenth level bard so if I want, I could summon an unseen servant—"

"Demon—what if I wanted to summon a demon?" Olivia's tone got serious as she cut off Percy before he could finish. "Or like, could any character *accidently* summon a demon?"

"Accidently?" Theresa asked, sounding confused. "I mean, usually summoning, especially a demon, would take a whole ass ritual, and you would have to have encountered certain NPC's and gained knowledge and—oh my god, I've completely lost you. I'm sorry."

"No. You're good," Olivia shook her head. She desperately wanted to know more without seeming too eager for answers, but it was hard to hide. "I just—I'm researching for this story I'm working on. I'm already kind of deep in it, but I can't figure out how my main character got into this demonic mess, and I feel like understanding the rules for this sort of thing might give me some clarity. Maybe?"

"Well," said Theresa, "the cool thing about writing your own stuff is, *you* get to make the rules but, I get it. So, if your main character summoned a demon *by accident* I'm assuming it's presence is unwanted?"

"Very."

"There's quite a difference between summoning and binding when it comes to demons," said Hector. "Perhaps your character inadvertently bound themselves. Or, was bound by outside forces and thus, they can't seem to get rid of this demon. Is the demon hunting or hurting your main character?"

"Kind of? It's more like, hunting *for* her… but she doesn't want it to."

"Sounds like it's bound in servitude. Interesting." Hector massaged his giant red beard.

Percy jumped in: "There's also, like, a lot of different types of demons. Greater demons, lesser demons, demonic constructs, demon lords, Deathdrinkers…"

"Is there such a thing as like, techno-demons? Cyber-demons? Is that a thing?"

"Oh snap," said Theresa. "You just said the magic words."

"What? Cyber-demon?"

"Techno. Anything technomancy related gets Firewall over here, harder than me drooling over my boyfriend," said Percy, pointing a thumb at Hector who was now leaned forward over the table, anxiously waiting his turn to speak.

"A techno-demon is most certaintly a thing," Hector started as he pushed back his glasses, sounding a bit overly excited and yet all-together serious, "only, it's mostly only found in homebrew games, but I mean, there are some who believe that technomancy is as real as black magick or witchcraft."

"*Aaaand* here we go…" said Percy, who picked up his phone and distracted himself once again.

"Homebrew? Like, beer?" asked Olivia.

"Homebrew as in, Hector doesn't like to go by the rulebooks so, he meticulously and endlessly spends all of his time crafting his own adventures, races, classes in a D&D inspired game that he is creating on his own," said Theresa.

Hector was beaming with pride. "Um, yes, I've been working on a game for a few years, *but* I've also been researching and studying just as meticulously! Some of this shit is real."

"Hector." Theresa tried to stop him before he went into a full on rant, but it was too late.

"Think about it. You've heard of positive reinforcement, right? What about quantum physics? You seen *The Secret* or *What the Bleep Do We Know?*"

Olivia returned a blank stare.

"Well, they're very popular and the whole idea behind them is the connection between quantum physics and the vibrations that we have, the vibrations that *everything* has, and how we can manipulate those vibrations. The frequencies that we all operate on. It's literally what connects us and everything around us. Computers, technology, cell phones, it's all tuned-in to a certain frequency as well. If we can manipulate that?" Hector gestured a tiny explosion out of the side of his head with his hand. "Real fucking magic dude." He grabbed his beer and took a celebratory chug, feeling quite pleased with himself. "I'm compiling somewhat of a technological grimoire that encapsulates all of this. I call it: the Techronomicon."

"Techronomicon? I like it," said Olivia.

"Oh man, you'll love it when it's done," said Hector before belching loudly. "Ugh. Sorry."

"You're fine." Olivia laughed. She twirled her beer bottle between her fingers on the table and hesitated before asking, "So, does your Techronomicon have a section on how to get rid of a techno demon?"

"Hmm. Yes and no, I'm still working on it but essentially... it would take a bit of legwork. These things are like the worst kind of malware. Hard to remove and even harder to permantly delete. Everytime you try, they just bury themselves deeper into your hardware. Perhaps, a metaphysical antivirus of sorts, a bigger, badder yet, more benevolent entity. Only, I don't know how one would go about summoning *that!*"

"Can we *please* talk about real life for a second?" cried Percy.

"Okay, okay," said Hector, "I need another beer anyways. I've been babysitting this thing for twenty minutes now. Oh! One more thing though, if your main character is trying to get rid of said demon, it helps to know it's name. Do you have a name for it yet?"

"Oh, she knows it's name. It's Render," said Olivia.

"Render?" asked Percy. "Like waiting for a picture to render?"

"How tech-y," said Theresa.

"I think it's more like — the act of rending, to tear something apart."

"Heart-rending, litterally. I like it," said Hector

"I dunno. Sounds kind of like Slender Man to me," said Percy indifferently.

"Very different," said Olivia. "Well, I mean, he does wear a suit too, but that's really the only other similarity. This thing is like Beetlejuice mixed with Max Headroom, Freddy Krueger, and T-1000 all rolled into one."

"Jesus," said Theresa, "you've really thought this thing out."

"Yeah," Olivia looked down at her hands, "I haven't been able to *stop* thinking about it."

"Wait," Hector snapped his fingers, "Render like the render virus from the early 2000's! Oh, my god, that is genius! That thing was a literal monster of a virus. Once you opened it up, it would just decimate your entire mainframe and then go after every single contact it could find a connection to in your system. Absolutely brutal. The only thing that would be left on your computer would be this pixelated image of this ghostly, well, pretty much exactly what Olivia described. Deep cut, man, very clever. Apparently, the guy that created it offed himself but I think the government took him out because he was too big a threat. Wild story."

Olivia gulped.

Hector continued, "Well, at any rate, for uh, storytelling purposes, by knowing the demon's true name you can ban—"

All at once Olivia's ears were engulfed by deafening static and high pitch ringing. Hector's face started collapsing in on itself like the distorted image from an old, damaged VHS tape. No one else seemed to notice; Percy was absent mindedly scrolling through his phone and when Olivia looked to her left to see if Theresa was sharing this horrid halucination, she caught Theresa gazing back at her intently. Theresa looked embarrased and flustered and took a long sip from her drink as she stared up at the ceiling. Olivia turned back to Hector whose face was still melting and imploding, her ears were swarming with metallic insect wings.

"What the fuck?" she shouted as her beer bottle slipped through her fingers and clanked loudly against the table, landing on it's side. The group shifted it's focus back to her. The noise in her ears ceased, and Hector's big fireball of a head went back to normal. Though, he did lift a hand to his temples and complain about a sudden headache.

"Uh, you okay?" asked Theresa.

"Yeah, you didn't see that? Sorry, I think maybe I've had one too many of these." She picked up the empty bottle.

Is it the weed again? Taylor's voice rang in her head. *Where is Taylor for that matter? How long have I been in here?*

She checked the time on her phone. She'd been away from Taylor for a few hours and it was starting to feel weird. She was very much enjoying the company and conversation but she hoped Taylor wasn't mad at her for quasi-ditching her at her own party.

Olivia looked around the kitchen and towards the crowded hallway to see if she could spot any sign of her best friend. From the distance she heard a familiar voice shouting her name. Taylor must have been thinking the exact same thing. They were constantly in sync during such moments.

"Oliviaaaaa! Olivia Peramo!"

Olivia got out of her chair as she saw her favorite confidant,

180 pounds of pluck mixed with poise and caramel complexion, muscling her way through the sea of house guests, and clearly tipsier than Olivia. She burst into the kitchen and almost tackled her friend.

"There you are, you giant smelly C-word!"

"Whoah." Olivia chuckled and gave her friend a playful shove. "I was just about to go looking for you."

"Bitch, you better be! Do you not hear what's playing right now?"

Olivia hadn't even noticed the music for the entirety of her kitchen conversations. She stopped to listen and immediately noticed the distinctive warbling underwater guitar riffs of the intro to their favorite "Mom made me listen to this song so many times that I love it now" song of their childhood; "Come Undone" by Duran Duran.

Olivia screamed with glee. Taylor squealed back at her. Olivia turned to the table and yelled to the G(r)eek Squad over her shoulder as Taylor pulled her out of the room. "I'll see you guys later! Super nice meeting you!"

They ran to the living room to dance and play air guitar as they traded off reciting the lyrics back and forth. They went through every step of the dance they had made up for their fifth grade talent show and laughed until they could hardly breathe. They didn't care who was watching. They didn't care whether or not the guests were judging, laughing, or participating. Olivia did not give a single shit. Times like this, it was just the two of them. Their own nearly impenetrable world, invisible to the realm of the living. Olivia cherished the seconds, however fleeting they were.

Until the music stopped.

Olivia felt every eye in the room. Every judgemental, awkward, half-smile. She was suddenly giving out every shit that she had.

Taylor could sense the dread swelling up inside of Olivia. "Babe. Hey. Look at me." She brushed a stray blonde hair away from her eyes. "You good?"

Olivia's head started throbbing. She wasn't sure if it was from her anxiety or the alcohol or a combination of both. She only knew she needed to get out of the room before it started spinning.

"I'm fine," she lied. "Just, really need to pee," she said hurredly, giving Taylor a not-so-reassuring smile and making a b-line for the restroom. Olivia grabbed onto the edges of the bathroom sink as she stared at herself in the mirror. Deep breaths helped alleviate the itchy wool sweater feeling inside her chest. If she were being honest with herself, she was surprised she had made it this long into the night without making her routine escape to the bathroom to breathe. It happened at every party, at least once. Even small family gatherings and kick-backs. She really did love to mingle and see her friends and family, but something about forced small talk and overdoses of social inter-action, no matter how near and dear the third party may be, always made Olivia feel slightly claustrophobic. When she had arrived at Taylor's home this evening, in light of recent events, she figured she would be spending half the night in the bath-room.

"Get a grip, kid," she quoted Alejandro's constant advice to her reflection. She ran the sink and scooped a small handfull of water into her mouth. Wiping her chin with the back of her jacket sleeve, she gazed into her own tiger-striped eyes. That's what her father had always called them. He said they reminded him of his favorite gem stone, Tiger's-Eye. She watched herself carefully, as if she might catch her reflection slipping up and making a slight movement that she hadn't made on her side. Her ears filled with white noise as she focused on herself and zoned out of everything around her.

Who are you?

Why are you like this?

Why can't you just be fearless and maliable like Taylor? Why can't you let go like Ally told you to? For once, Olivia Peramo, just be brave. You can write, read, watch, eat, breathe, bleed Horror and yet... Virtually everything in real life scares the shit out of you. I

*know you never wanted to do anything alone, but now you fucking
have to. Taylor can't always swoop in to rescue you. She won't always
have time for you.*

*You can do this. You can beat this. It's never going to stop being
scary, but if you don't take those first steps, it's never going to stop.
Period. Think about how well you did in school. Think about conquer-
ing the forest with Ally. Think about every succesful story you've
ever posted. Just do what you do best, besides hiding in someone else's
bathroom. Throw on some blinders, light a torch and run screaming
into the night. Kick the ass of whatever obstacle you face. Like you
always do. For Taylor. For Alejandro. For Mom and Dad. For Mimi.
For yourself.*

Olivia took another second and said a mini prayer. She
wasn't necessarily religious, but she was overly superstitious.
She thanked her brother and her father and Taylor too, for
every pep-talk they ever crammed inside of her thick skull. She
wouldn't be able to psych herself without them. She mimed a
tiny cross over her face and said *amen.*

The world around her came back into frame and she took
a listen. She could her a muffled sultry voice sneaking underneath the bathroom door. Sounded like Lana Del Rey but she
wasn't sure. The music cut out abruptly. Olivia emerged from
the bathroom to see who or what cut the chord.

"Um... Taylor?" Michael was standing rigidly next to the
entertainment system with his finger on the pause button. He
was half smiling, half grimacing. "Care to join us on the lanai
for a toast, honey?"

Taylor looked like a startled teenager, caught redhanded
smoking something they shouldn't by a dissapointed father.
She looked at Olivia out of the corner of her eye and did her
absolute best not to burst out laughing. Michael looked allto-
gether annoyed and embarassed. Taylor looked down shyly,
cleared her composure and looked back at her fiancee.

"Of course, babe." She turned to Olivia before following
Michael out of the room. "Come on Olly, let's see to the...
lanaiiii," said Taylor in her best Robin Leach accent.

EIGHT

AFTER THE TOASTS AND THE speeches came cake, more wine, and some champagne. Most of the guests had filtered out and said their goodbyes. By the tail end of the night, the party had dwindled down to a bodycount of thirteen. Michael's youngest cousin, a handful of his college buddies, the G(r)eek Squad, Taylor, Michael, and Olivia all huddled in wicker chairs surrounding a rippling fire pit in the lanai. The warmth from the fire was doing its best to disarm the bitter cold wafting in through the screened-in walls. The light from the pool behind them reflected its tranquil waves dancing across the ceiling. The music had switched to a blend of laid back lofi hip-hop instrumentals. The atmosphere was hypnotically intoxicating for the inebriated. Two bottles of red wine made their way around the circle. Taylor leaned over and handed one to Olivia.

"Oh, I don't have a glass."

"So? Drink from the bottle, Smelly."

"Stupid," Olivia replied before taking a swig.

Hector, who had passed out in a papason chair, let out a

monstrous snore. Jason slapped him awake.

"What the fu—" Hector mumbled in a drunken stupor.

"Come on, big man. I think it's time we hit the road," said Jason, getting up from his chair.

Percy followed suit and helped Hector up and on his feet. The trio turned to Theresa, who was still seated next to Olivia.

"You coming?" asked Jason.

"No I rode my pegasus, remember? I'm going to stay for a bit. The Dragon Wagon will have to ride sans its fair maiden tonight."

Olivia giggled at her nerd-talk. Theresa blushed.

"Suit yourself, Thereseus," Jason replied. "Nice meeting you all. Michael and Taylor we wish you the absolute best of luck. See you for the wedding!"

The three of them began walking away before Hector jerked to a stop and threw one meaty index finger in the air. "Stidgy Stewy!"

"Oh, come on, mate," said Jason, sounding exasperated. "You've got to know your limits. Let's g—"

"No you fuggin—" Hector pushed Jason off of his shoulder. "Stitch stewardess."

"I... are you trying to say *Stygian Stewardess*?" asked Olivia, who was just noticing more than a few pairs of confused eyes around the fire. "It's uh, my online monocre," she admitted bashfully.

Hector slowly turned around to face the remaining party goers. He stretched out his finger and pointed at Olivia. He made a noise that sounded like he swallowed his own barf and contiued: "Yesh. No! 'Livia... it's, it's not you."

"I am so confused right now."

"It's not the weed either!" Hector grunted oafishly.

"What—"

"It's real. He's a real thing," Hector whispered loudly through his teeth.

"Firewall, buddy, I don't think anyone here gets what you're going for." Theresa laughed nervously.

Olivia knew exactly where he was going though, and her stomach sank before he even got there. She could feel it coming.

"Renderrrrr!" Hector growled in an animalistic tone. The flames from the fire pit flickered in the reflection of Hector's glasses. He looked like a burning sun, wobbling back and forth, threatening to fall out of his own orbit at any second. "You gotta *hic* gotta banish 'im. B—banishing ritual... and..." Hector slapped a hand over his own mouth. His cheeks ballooned out and it was suddenly obvious that he was harboring a mouthful of his own vomit.

"Oh no. You are not doing that in here sweety," said Percy, as he quickly grabbed Hector by the arm. "I'll take him outside. Lovely to see you guys! Jason? Can you start the van? Let's G-T-F-O before Mount Vesuvius here erupts, please! Bye, guys!" They rushed him out of the house and left ten befuddled faces sitting around the fire. Michael's college buddies were howling with laughter. Taylor whipped around and looked at Olivia with wide eyes.

"You told them?" she asked quietly. It was a small circle of people however and anyone who wasn't still laughing could have easily heard her. Olivia looked at the rest of the crowd then back to Taylor.

"Uh, yeah?" she stammered. "I told them, about the *story* I'm writing."

"Got it." Taylor nodded knowingly.

Olivia realized she was still holding the wine bottle. She took another pull and passed it off to her right.

"Well, that was, uh, interesting," came a voice to Olivia's right. The voice's owner placed a hand over Olivia's fingers as she passed him the bottle.

She quickly withdrew her hand and leaned in the opposite direction, towards Taylor. She gave the mystery man her strongest *"um Hi, who the fuck are you?"* look that she could muster but she was quite drunk, so it ended up looking more flirtatious than confrontational.

"Sorry, I don't think we were ever properly introduced. I'm

Ron. Ron Mitchell. Mike's brother from another mother, if you will, and hopefully, soon-to-be best man, right?" He joked as he jabbed Michael in the rib with a sharp elbow.

Olivia was super unimpressed, not only by his college boy "charm" and smug demeanor but also by his slicked back haircut and too-flashy-to-not-be-a-flex suit. Drunk or not, she thought it looked stupid.

Taylor leaned over stealthily and whispered (with some actual discretion this time), "This is the guy I wanted you to meet. Isn't he cute?" She poked Olivia's side.

Olivia whispered back through clenched teeth, "He looks like McLovin cosplaying a very shitty Vincent Vega."

"Olivia!" said Taylor just a tad too loud as she pushed her friend's shoulder.

"What happened? Did I miss something?" asked Ron with a shit-eating grin.

"No. We, um, we were just saying... uh, where's that bottle?" Olivia was too gone to come up with any kind of cover and desperately wanted something to give her an excuse to not have to talk.

Theresa got out of her seat and grabbed the bottle that someone had placed near the edge of the fire pit instead of keeping it circulating.

"Ah, somebody's fuckin' up the rotation!" yelled Olivia as Theresa walked the bottle over to her. "Thank you, love! You are my favorite person I have met tonight."

Theresa brushed a hair behind her ear and smiled, "Like-wise, m'lady." She bowed awkwardly and returned to her seat.

"So, what was that dude even talking about? Who are we trying to banish?" asked Ron.

"Nobody knows, Ron Mitchell," said Olivia, leaning a bit heavy on the sarcasm.

"Well, if you need somebody gone, I dunno if Mikey or Taylor told you this, but I was a bouncer for six years. I've been known to banish some bitches in my time, right Mikey?"

Even Michael looked embarassed by his friend. "Right."

"Well, Ron Mitchell, you might be surprised to hear this but until tonight, I've never even heard of you before. And six years? Wow! That is an impressive amount of time to hold such a menial job." Olivia sat back in her chair and killed the rest of the wine bottle.

Theresa stifled an audible laugh. Ron shifted uncomfortably in his seat.

"Olivia Peramo! Be nice!" Taylor shouted at her.

"No, it's cool, you're fine, she's fine. I think I come off a little arrogant sometimes. I probably deserved that," Ron said as he tugged his sleeve over the watch on his wrist.

Olivia tucked in her chin and laughed to herself muttering, "A little?" under her breath.

"Olly!" Taylor slapped Olivia's knee. Olivia turned to her and made a face, keeping her chin tucked in and sticking out her front teeth.

Ron laughed to himself and brushed it off. "What did that guy call you, Stitchy Studious?"

"Stygian Stewardess," said Olivia, Theresa, and Taylor, all correcting him at the same time.

"Ahhh!" Olivia shouted as she gave both her new friend and old friend high fives.

"Ohhh… Stygian as in, the river Styx, extremely dark or gloomy?"

Olivia was a bit taken aback.

Theresa, on the other hand, was underwhelmed. "Okay, that's literally the Miriam Webster definition. You just have that stored in your memory?"

"No, I um, looked it up," he said, holding up his phone's screen. Michael and his buddies laughed while the girls rolled their eyes.

"Ron is actually, not always a d-bag," said Taylor in a sisterly sort of way, "He's usually super sweet and focused and he is doing *very well* with his big new Hollywood job."

Ron looked embarassed but emboldened. "Not Hollywood yet, but, if I play my cards right… I just might be an associate at a *very* big production company come this May."

"That's my boy!" yelled Michael as he slapped Ron's back.

Taylor raised her eyebrows at Olivia, who returned a slight nod before dazing off into the fire pit.

How is she not reading me at all with this guy? Why does she always get such a hard-on for these wannabe badass fratboy business types?

"Stygian Stewardess, huh? I like it. It's dark, mysterious, fits the whole—" Ron waved his hands around in the air. "...vibe you got going. It's hot."

His smile made Olivia cringe. She'd rather have seen Render's sickly grin full of little pearly white caskets. She bit her tongue and simply replied, "Thank you, Ron Mitchell."

"RonnieReallyWrites, Ronnie with an 'ie', if you want to look me up on Twitter."

"Oh, I don't believe in Twitter," she lied. "Social constructs are—"

"This you?" Ron held up his phone again, showing Olivia's Twitter profile.

Shit. I suck at lying when I'm drunk.

Wait, what the fuck is that?

"Uh, can I see that again?" Olivia asked, sitting fully upright in her chair.

"Yeah... that *is* you right?"

"No, I mean, yeah. But what is all..." Olivia took Ron's phone out of his hands and started scrolling through her own feed. "I only posted once the other day, this is..."

She scrolled and scrolled. Somehow her account had sent out the same tweet hundreds of times. The only difference in each tweet was every message became progressively more corrupted and broken than the last. The font glitched so wildly that the most recent of them was barely even legible. Olivia's hair felt like a wool cap as her scalp overheated. She brushed her behind her ears as panic set in and a rock formed in her gut.

"Hacked? I think I got hacked! I didn't post all that crazy shit." Olivia felt the alcohol in her system swinging from her chandalier of a brain.

"I thought it was some sort of spooky, witchy gimmick you were going for I—"

"It's not a fucking gimmick, dude," Olivia shot back. "Ugh, I feel sick." She threw Ron Mitchell's phone back into his lap and reclined in her seat as she placed a hand on her forehead.

"I can give you a ride home if you want?" said Theresa. "My pegasus, er—my motorcycle, has a side car. I was about to head out anyways."

"Oh, you're so sweet girl, but I think I might just crash here tonight. Think I need to sleep this off."

"No worries. Hope you feel better. I had a great time tonight, guys. Congrats again! Olivia, it was awesome meeting you," said Theresa as she made her exit.

"You're an amazing warrior woman and I already love your face!" shouted Olivia, her hand still covering her eyes.

Michael gave Taylor a concerned look. Taylor put her hand on Olivia's shoulder and spoke to her softly: "Hon' you know I love you but, Mike's cousin Greg already passed out on the couch…"

"It's okay, Taytay, I'll just curl up right here." Olivia pulled up her legs and rolled herself into a fetal position. "I'm so… so tired."

"Olly, you're gonna freeze to death out here once the fire's out."

"Babe. I'm good. I'm a cold-ass bitch, 'member? Colder than death itself," she hissed with her eyes shut tight.

She heard Taylor laugh followed by the muffled sound of her and Michael fighting in hushed tones. The lofi hip-hop drums slowed to a snail's pace, and the world faded to black as Olivia drifted off to sleep.

NINE

1995 WAS ONE OF THE hottest summers in recent years for Missouri. Luckily the ice cream man had made his rounds today, and not just the regular ice cream man in the little blue truck. Today, they got a visit from the *good* ice cream man in the big yellow van. The yellow van ice cream man always had the best of the best. Every flavor of ice pop, every ice cream character with bubble gum eyes, and a few extra that the sad little blue truck never had in stock. Yellow van man also had *all* the candy, even the candy they weren't supposed to buy, like bubblegum cigarettes and those test tube vials of pure sugar in different colors and flavors. On top of that, he had the secret stuff, the stuff he kept hidden when concerned parents were standing over their kid's shoulder. Stink bombs, fart bombs (*yes* there was a difference), smoke bombs, gun powder caps and cap guns... everything a meddlesome youth could possibly think of. He was like Willy Wonka mixed with Uncle Buck in a big banana cream hippie bus.

Olivia sat on the large green metal box across the street

from her home that housed an electrical transformer, despite the multiple warning signs advising against it. She couldn't be bothered to care. She had a grape Mickey Mouse popsicle in one hand and her stuffed Stay-Puft Marshmallow Man tucked under her other arm. The heat was sweltering and she was uncomfortably sticky, but it was too nice a day to complain. She watched as Alejandro and his friends tossed colored smoke bombs at each other, emitting cloudy funnels that choked the air in a blue and red haze. They fired cap guns back and forth and acted out dramatic deaths on the sidewalk.

A small tickling sensation crept over her kneecap. Olivia looked down and spotted a quarter-sized spider crawling up her leg. For a second, she froze in fear, but as she stared down at the arachnid, it honestly felt harmless. It wasn't black nor red so, no black widow. It was brown and furry, and Olivia wasn't sure if that was a good thing or a bad thing, but the more she looked at it, the cuter it became to her. She left it alone and continued watching the neighborhood wars. Her leg jumped as the spider made it's way higher up her thigh. It suddenly felt bigger, heavier. Olivia looked down again and saw no longer a small fuzzy spider, but a gargantuan tarantula. It was drumming its thick arachnid legs against her thigh and trying to make its way under her shorts. Now, Olivia was frozen for real, she tried to jump but she was stuck. Her back was pressed against something sticky and leathery.

It wasn't 1995. It was present day, and Olivia was no longer asleep in a comfy wicker chair in Taylor's lanai. She was laying down in the humid backseat of a BMW. She immediately felt sick to her stomach and her head pounded. She could faintly hear an Orville Peck song coming from the radio in the car, some slow cowboy love song that sounded like Elvis Presly singing Morrisey lyrics. The tarantula was still riding up her leg, getting dangerously close to her crotch.

Olivia opened her eyes and looked down. Everything was fuzzy; it was still dark out. A shadowy figure loomed over her lower half. She rubbed her eyes and held back the urge to vomit. Blinking, she looked back down the length of her body and realized there was no tarantula, only the hairy knuckled hands of Ron Mitchell skating their way under her one good party dress.

"What the fffuck?" Olivia mustered in a groggy voice.

Ron pulled his hand back and slowly climbed on top of her. "Shh-shh-shh…" He put a finger to Olivia's lips. "I know you couldn't take your eyes off me tonight. I couldn't take mine off of you either."

Olivia was genuinely baffled. The night was a bit of a blur towards the end but she was positive that she had not sent a single message in Ron's general direction even once that night. If she had looked at him at all it was with ill contempt.

How the hell did he get me here? Why didn't Taylor stop him?

Olivia's body writhed underneath his but she could hardly move. She didn't understand how someone that looked so feeble could weigh so much.

Is this scumbag really going to try and take me? God he stinks like a musky bag of golf clubs!

The smell of his cologne clogged her throat. Ron leaned in to kiss her, and Olivia's head shot up, smashing her forehead against his. She shoved him out of the way and began retching and heeving puddles of beer, cake, and red wine onto the floor of his backseat. Ron cupped his face as he reeled backwards.

"What the fuck?" Ron barked.

"What the fuck, me?" shouted Olivia, gasping for air and wiping the slimy strings of spit from her mouth. "What the fuck, *you*?"

Clutching the side of the seat, she lifted her left leg and kicked Ron right in the dick with her heel. Ron tumbled out of the car, falling onto his back in the dirt. He rolled back and forth holding his junk and writhing in pain. Olivia staggered out of the opposite door and held on to the car while she walked around to the back.

Ron scrambled to his knees and let out a whiny growl. "You'll pay for that, you bitch!" He slowly rose to his feet.

Olivia looked around to figure out her surroundings. Dirt, tall grass, no street lights, a thicket of trees not too far in the distance. She was near her neighborhood. She recognized this distinct stretch of rural road. She knew there wasn't a house or a business for at least a mile.

Ron pounced on her and pinned her against the car. His slick black hair hung wild, his eyes shaking as he frothed at the mouth. He pressed his repugnant lips against her ear. "I know what bad girls like you really want." His breathing was ragged and hot. He slid a hand around her throat and squeezed hard.

Olivia was terrified but did her best not to show it. She wondered how many girls Ron Mitchell had already taken adavantage of in this drunken state. She wished she hadn't had so much to drink, though she was feeling plenty sobered after ejecting her own weight in vomit. Sober enough at least to make a calculated move. Olivia dropped her guard and pretended to feign interest for a half second before screaming, "Fuck you Mitchell!" and sending a knee into his groin, decimating his undercarriage yet again. Ron doubled over in pain and growled some more.

Olivia screamed at him, "I'm nothing like the girls you know, you lame-ass! Couldn't get a real date to save your life, rapist!"

Ron slowly stood, seething and trembling. The look in his eyes was boiling rage. The sound of buzzing wasps seemed to fill the roadway. Ron hunched his back, readying himself to spring into another attack but stopped with a jerk.

His eyes widened and a single stream of blood dripped from the side of his mouth. Ron clambered forward one step before falling flat on his face. Standing directly behind him was Render.

It was the first time Olivia had seen him face to face that wasn't a dream. The red glow from Ron's tail lights illuminated his terrible visage. She had thought it was just a hideous Halloween mask when she saw him on the computer but now it looked real, fleshy and cold.

"No! No, no, no…" Olivia whimpered quietly. She realized her mouth was trembling. The sticky slime of residual puke seemed to thicken on her tongue, tasting increasingly more grotesque with each beat of her throbbing heart

He needed to get what he deserved but he didn't need to fucking die!

Olivia wanted to scream at the ghoul but she was afraid of drawing Render's ire upon herself. Olivia wanted to run but she wasn't sure she could move.

I had it under control, you fucking psycho! she screamed internally. Her stomach churned as she watched the cybernetic monstrosity. She felt helpless and sick. Her body ached from the oncoming hangover festering in her guts.

Render looked at Olivia and shook his head, emitting a series of clicking noises and static. Then, in a flash, Render was kneeling down over Ron's limp body, pulling out his switch blade and stabbing him over and over again. The motions were so quick and robotic in nature, it looked like a sewing machine in reverse, tearing Ron Mitchell apart at the seems. Olivia was overcome with revulsion — her mind and body clattered against each other like a machine with broken gears.

Render's face was drenched in Ron's blood. It shone a deep obsidian shade of crimson in the red luminescence of the tail lights. The smell of it swirled into the air with the dirt and Ron's cologne, and the stench of what Olivia left in his back seat.

As soon as Olivia got a whiff, everything that was left in her stomach came up. She sprayed the ground with her dinner and wobbled as she stood back up. Her head throbbed and pins and needles ran through her body. Olivia tried with every ounce of her being to stay coherent but her eyes rolled back in her head and she blacked out, falling hard to the ground...

TEN

OLIVIA AWOKE THE NEXT MORNING, safe at home in her bed. Her hangover was kicking her ass and she was having a hell of a time trying to recollect the string of events from the previous night.

Was that another dream? Sure felt real as hell. How on Earth did I get home, and who put me in my bed? So, what? Does this freaking Frankenstein monster have a thing for me?

Why didn't he kill me?

Olivia pulled her sludge-filled body out of bed and assessed herself. She was still wearing the same clothes. Her legs were definitely stained with dirt and something... grimy. Her neck still hurt from when Ron had grabbed her by the throat.

Oh shit.

Oh no.

If that was real... Ron is fucking dead and my DNA is literally everywhere!

Oh-shit, Oh-shit, Oh-shit!

Wait.

Am I – am I doing this? Is Render my Tyler Durden?

Right. I'm in fucking **Fight Club** *and I'm a serial killer now… Congratulations, Olivia, you have officially snapped your little ADHD-addled brain in twain.*

"Ugh…What did I do?" she groaned.

Olivia picked up her phone and scrolled through her missed calls and texts, all from Taylor:

"Where did you disappear to, Smelly!?"

"OMG did you leave with Ron, you whore???"

"Answer meeeeeeee"

"Booooo!"

"K seriously Olly?

starting to worry.

but I know you're okay.

but I still want you to call me.

NOW!"

"Herro??"

"You don't have to take the walk of shame alone; I can pick you up…"

"SMELLYYYYYYYYYYYYYYYYYY!"

Olivia mulled over what to write her friend for a good thirty minutes before finally sending:

"At home. Took an Uber."

"Didn't see Ron when I left."

"Hungover as a mother."

"Ow."

"Love you."

She was afraid to tell the details of what little she remembered. Afraid of making herself an accomplice and afraid of sounding like a complete psychopath, again. She knew she would have to tell Taylor at some point; keeping things from Taylor was nearly impossible for Olivia. Not because Taylor was any sort of detective, but because Olivia really had no one else to tell, and if she kept something inside, it was inevitable that it would fester and bubble until she couldn't stand it a minute more and all the words would just come pouring out.

Which reminded her, the vomit in Ron Mitchell's car. If anyone found that at the scene of the crime, she'd undoubtedly become the prime suspect. She grabbed her laptop and started googling every local news site she could find—but maybe it was too early. Had anyone even stumbled upon his chewed-up corpse yet? Olivia grabbed her car keys and decided to investigate herself. She made the decision, regardless of what she saw, she must keep driving.

She took a quick shower and changed into an oversized Linkin Park hoodie and some cozy sweatpants before hopping into her car. She sped down the road, looking for signs of the location that she remembered. After driving around a long, forested bend, she came to the corner of the tree line and the exact spot where she remembered everything happening. She slowed to a crawl as she passed by.

There was nothing there. No car. No body. No cops or forensics. Olivia disobeyed her own ultimatum, came to a full stop, and got out of the car. Not even a drop of blood in the dirt.

Okay? Okay. How drunk was I last night? I was pretty fucking drunk. This one was just another bad dream then, right? A real shovel to the back of the head hangover with fangs kind of fucked up dream.

Right?

Flashes of Ron Mitchell's destruction popped into her mind. She rubbed her hand against her neck while bits and pieces came and went. Orville Peck singing about falling roses ear-wormed its way into her brain and she wanted to throw up all over again. Last time she dreamt about Render it had felt uncannily real. Could it be another dream? That didn't explain the bruise on her neck or the bits of God-knows-what she woke up with on her legs.

Olivia looked up at the sky. Sun rays pierced through her skull and thumped against her brain with the force of an over-powered subwoofer. The heat piled itself on her chest and her back in dense layers of sweat. Gone were the gray clouds and the rain from the last few days and all that was left was the humidity and soggy leaves on the side of the road, slowly drying out into brittle skeletons of what once was. Olivia jumped back in her car and blasted the air conditioning. She dialed up Taylor on the telephone and sped home like she was trying to outrun her own hangover.

"Fucking finally!" Taylor answered.

"Hey."

"What happened to you? I'm so mad at you by the way. I was bringing you waffles and this whole pretty little plate this morning and lo and behold... you dipped on me in the middle of the night without even a note or anything!"

"A note?"

"A text, a call? I don't know, fucking something!"

"Sorry. Sorry. Sorryyyy!"

"Whatever." Taylor's tone was dismissive. "You okay?"

"Yeah, yeah. I mean. I think? I honestly have no idea how I got home."

"You sure you didn't get a ride with Ronnie boy?"

"Positive." Olivia covered for herself.

"Well, your car wasn't here when I checked. Maybe you pulled a College-Olly move and just drove yourself home while still blacked out?"

"How is that College-Olly? I drove drunk *once* in college, and it was because *you* had alcohol poisoning. But... it is weird that my car was with me... I didn't even think about it till now and I am literally sitting inside of my car."

"Yeesh. How you feelin? And why are you back in your car this early?"

Olivia groaned as she rubbed her eyes until she could see colorful sparks on the inside of her eyelids, "I—I had to... run an errand, kind of... and feel like a 120 lb. bag of dogshit—thank you for asking."

"Okay well, go get you a giant plate of greasy ass food, preferably Chuck-A-Burger, and smoke some more of your pots and fucking get some sleep! Rest your pretty head homegirl. That thing has been in too many places lately. You need a break."

"I know. Thank you. I will."

"K-k. I love you."

"I love you too, Taytay."

Olivia ended the call and headed inside her home. She didn't feel like eating anything. She didn't feel like smoking either. Sleep sounded nice but even as worn out as she felt, she was too afraid of falling into another Nightmare on Render Street. Olivia trudged through her house and before she even realized where she was walking, she was folding her legs in a pretzel and taking a seat at her computer desk.

ELEVEN

THERE WAS A LARGE CUP of ice water next to Olivia that she didn't remember procuring in the slightest, but she was incredibly grateful for its existence.

She took to her usual haunts on the internet and remembered the bit from last night where Ron exposed her spambot-esque Twitter vomit. She clicked over to her profile to make sure it wasn't just another part of her dream. Sure enough, it was all there. As far as she could scroll, hundreds of tweets, all variations of the initial summoning circle tweet. The most recent one was so distorted it looked like she had dumped the text into a digital meat grinder.

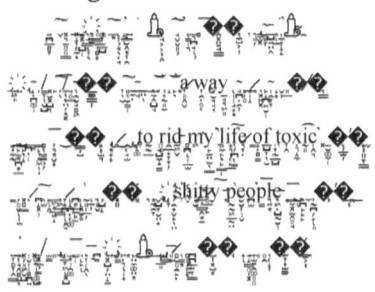

It took Olivia almost an hour to scrub every one of them, and the original deluge of cryptic posts had cost her at least twenty followers. Nobody wants their feed clogged up with spam, especially if it's some sort of edgy self-promo for your scary stories. She was embarrassed that she hadn't noticed it sooner. She would have unfollowed herself too.

Olivia chugged half her glass of water and closed her eyes, mentally pushing her headache down into a tiny hidden pocket so she could go about her day without the feeling of her brain treating her skull the way the incredible Hulk treated a fresh pair of shorts. As she opened her eyes her desktop came into focus. One icon stood out from the others; a video media icon with the title "PaloAlto07.16.03_R".

"The fuck did you come from?" Olivia asked the computer file. In the pit of her stomach there was an uneasy feeling that told her exactly where the file had come from, but she didn't want to believe it. Right clicking the icon, she selected "Play Video" from the drop-down menu.

The video began playing and the pit of her stomach did a somersault as her intuition confirmed its previous assertions. It was the original Render video. The one LTL had described to her, the very same one she knew from the heavily edited clips she had seen on the news in high school. Her gut reaction was to delete it immediately and hurl her computer into the fucking ether but, something deeper down compelled her to watch.

Every time you teeter on the edge of making a terrible decision, down beneath your queasy guts and anxious, shaky bones, there lies an indelible demon of will that pokes and prods at the very essence of your being until you force yourself to ignore the trepidation in your brain and just do the damn thing. Olivia was giving in to that very demon now. She couldn't get it to shut the hell up. She was already well on her way up shit's creek with all of this anyway. Why fight it now?

The video was almost word for word as LTL had described it in his lengthy email. It wasn't exceptionally long but watching it felt like it took an eternity. Every time. Olivia replayed the video multiple times. There were three things that jumped out to her:

1. Jay Holloway seemed incredibly suspicious and even mumbled quietly to himself toward the end of the video, "It wasn't supposed to work like this." Clearly, he had something more to do with Render's inception than he let on in the video.

2. The chatbot dialog had been from the night prior to the recording of the video and only invoked the creation of a corrupted link. But as Holloway poured over the chat log, he quietly read their words to himself as he went, and only after he had recited the chant out loud did things start going haywire; only then did Render appear.

3. The invocation ended with the line "b0und only by th3 darkness of y0ur host."

That third little nugget made her think back to the horrid apparition of Alejandro she had witnessed in her car and something that he had said to her: "Just please, please don't let your darkness consume you."

She could still hear his voice in her head, clear as day. Maybe it was a warning. Maybe he knew what was coming.

That, or I really need to get my goddamn head checked. This is probably all me being the world's most gullible asshole and buying in to some augmented reality game, and the creators are all laughing their freaking heads off right now.

Her thoughts wandered from pensive and worried to pissed off and indignant. How could two chatbots using turn-of-the-century technology summon a cyber-demon on their own? At a time no less, when the internet and artificial intelligence in general were both basically in their adolescent stages. If that really was the case then it had to go deeper. There had to be more hands in the pot. Something or someone more sinister working in the background. At the same time, if this was really all a well plotted play and she was the puppet on center stage, then whoever was pulling the strings could go straight to Hell.

She clicked out of the video and opened up her music player. "Mommy, What's a Gravedigga?" by the Gravediggaz popped up first, and she let it ride. The laid-back, jazzy guitar from the instrumental did wonders to quell her anger and massage the headache that kept creeping back in. A little weed and greasy food were starting to sound better and better. Olivia reached for the pipe and the jar full of Skywalker OG in her desk drawer. She placed a small nug in the bowl and started browsing the internet for the best fast food she could get delivered to her house.

I should really make something healthy; I've been eating like shit lately... She took her first hit and held it in as she continued her inner monologue, *Nah, too much work. Plus, I deserve to eat shit. If I can't be bothered to tolerate the stress of a normal life or process my own grief because I'm too stubborn. I mean, you are what you eat, right? I'm shit.*

She leaned in close to examine the tasty morsels gliding across her screen. For a bunch of food she considered shit, it sure didn't look or taste like it. Olivia had to pull her face away from the gravitational pull of the ads to notice that her phone had been dinging for the past few minutes.

Probably Taylor again. Oh shit, probably Vividh wondering where the hell I am!

Olivia scooped up her device but quickly realized it was neither Taylor nor Vividh.

DING!

The phone went off again in her hand, the vibration sending a shock up her arm. Every one of the messages had come from an unknown number, some sort of media file that she would have to unlock her phone to view. "Ugh," she droned, "no more media files." Begrudgingly, she opened her phone to see what it was. Sixteen of the exact same video file. She let the last one play.

It was a dash cam. No, a reverse camera? She could tell by the fisheye shape of the lens it was from the back of Ron Mitchell's car. The video was pixelated, and the sound was muffled.

At first, all she could see was the back of her dress and one of Ron Mitchell's legs as he pressed her up against the car. She could just barely make out her own voice yelling at him after watching her rocket-knee to the crotch and seeing Ron flying backward into the dirt. Olivia moved slightly out of frame, showing a full visual of Ron in all his rage, caked in digitized red light. It was dark but the lights from the car were just bright enough to make out what was happening.

She watched Ron get ready to pounce. She watched the life leave his eyes as Render appeared out of nowhere behind him. *Et tu Render?* The video glitched and broke apart as a rainbow wave passed over everything like an old VHS tape. When the camera focused again Render was kneeling over the limp body of Ron Mitchell. Stab after stab after stab. Ron's back became a fountain of gore. Render was absolutely covered in it. Olivia heard what sounded like a feeble squeak that she must have made herself. Then her body dropped to the ground.

Render stopped his needlework abruptly and walked towards Olivia's unconscious body. A buzzing noise grew louder and louder, the closer he got. By the time he reached Olivia, his face was in the camera and the buzz was so loud that it actually vibrated Olivia's phone. The screen faded into grainy static, and the video stopped on the distorted frame of Render's uncanny skeleton of a face.

Olivia didn't realize how hard she was breathing until the video ended. The headache slumped its way back into the front of her brain in full effect. Nothing made sense anymore. It was surreal. Then it wasn't real. Now it's 100% real. Real fucked up. Her head, her life, all of this was really, really fucked. She tried to steady her quaking as her hands held onto her phone.

Olivia swiped and deleted the entire conversation containing the video files.

DING.

DING.

DING.

Every time she deleted it, a new message popped up.

She tried to call the number that the messages were coming from but all she got was a loud dial tone and a robotic *"We're sorry, the number you've dialed is incorrect. Please hang up and try again."*

She sent a text: "Leave me the fuck. Alone."

The messages stopped coming.

Olivia paused for a second, her heart pounding. She thought hard about every weird ass-backwards moment that she'd experienced in the last two days. Hector's drunken ramblings flashed through her mind.

She sent another text: "I banish you Render. You have no place here. Go back to where or what the fuck you came from. K?"

Another moment of silence passed before the screen on her phone glitched and mashed all of its pixels together. The lights in Olivia's room flashed in every color of the rainbow. The television screen turned off and on. Her computer played the original Render video on its own as the volume shot up and blew out her speakers. Outside of her room, she heard more electronics freaking out throughout her home.

Olivia clasped her hands over her ears and screamed, "Stop!"

This time, Render wasn't listening. Chaos unraveled in every corner of the Peramo household. Olivia grabbed her phone and her laptop, shoving them into an old Jansport backpack. She rushed out of her room. The lights and the noise, though intangible, felt like they were physically assaulting her at every turn. The theme song from *The Office* was blaring from the TV in the living room, from beyond the closed door of Alejandro's old room the deadened bass of an Aesop Rock song was thumping against the floor like a Warhammer. The car alarms in both her parents' cars wailed from the garage.

Olivia's head throbbed, and she feared her ears might begin to bleed from the pressure. She wanted to crumple into a ball and cry or scream or both, but she had to keep moving. She swiped her car keys and made a b-line for the front door as the utter pandemonium battered the walls of her home.

Before she reached the exit, she stopped and whirled around toward the garage door. Olivia hated seeing those old relics, reminders of everything she lost, but she knew there was a small glimmer of hope lying underneath the seat of her dad's Taurus. She charged inside and muscled her way into of her dad's car as the horn honked ceaselessly and the sirens from her mother's car shrieked at her from the opposite side of the garage. Olivia reached around wildly under the driver's seat until she finally felt a cold lump of steel in her hand.

Bingo.

Olivia unlatched the restraints and pulled out her father's Ruger GP100. It was heavier than expected, but it gave her a small sense of comfort and protection. It was like holding her father's hand again for the first time since he left this Earth.

Stashing the gun in her waistband, she bolted out of the garage and back toward the front door. She ran outside and slammed the door behind her. Her father's gun fell out of her waistband with a loud *CLUNK*. She scrambled to pick it back up and hide it in her bag while she looked around frantically, making sure no neighbors were watching.

She locked the front door of her house and ran to her car. Before getting in, she stopped and turned to listen. Everything had stopped.

What is happening? What is the purpose of torturing me like this? Don't I torture myself enough already?

Olivia contemplated going back inside but decided against it. She had been through more than enough of the funhouse her life was turning into.

She dialed her best friend once more as she got into her Camry and took off.

"Hey, Taylor, I'm coming back to your house."

"Oh — okay. C'mon over, were just cleaning up a bit — "

"I might need — is it okay if I sleep over tonight?"

"Um, yeah, of course. Are you okay, hon?"

"No. Not at all."

Olivia turned off her phone and tossed it into her passenger seat, next to the Jansport. She turned off the car's sound system. Flying down the highway in silence the entire drive to Taylor's house.

TWELVE

"TAYLOR. AGAIN? BABE. WE CAN'T just take her in like a stray dog every time she has another mental break-down." Michael threw a hand in the air as he carried a large trash bag across their kitchen.

"A stray dog? Are you fucking kidding me, Michael?" Taylor looked across the kitchen table like she was about to jump over it and open-hand slap her fiancée back to the Reagan era.

"Look. I'm sorry. I know she's your best friend. I love her too, you know. I at least *have* love for her in my heart." Taylor's expression was not changing. "But you have to admit... She's a bit of an energy vampire. She *is*, babe! Every time you hang out — hell, every time you so much as talk to her on the phone — you end up drained and all sad because her malaise affects you. Because that's the type of person you are. You want to save every abandoned puppy you see and fix whatever damaged goods you can. And I love that about you. It just hurts me to see you getting dragged down by it. I mean, I know she's had a fucked-up couple of years—I get it. But she needs to learn how to get over it. She needs to move on." He was shouting now. "Sell that house for Christ's sake. Spend some of that inheritance on herself. That's the crazy part, she has no excuse to keep bumming off you for rides. Well okay, not anymore, but even getting that car was like you were pulling her teeth. And she bums off of you for emotional support as well, babe. It's not fair to us—you. It's not fair to you."

"Of course, she uses me for emotional support, Michael," Taylor shouted back. "She's basically my fucking sister. She can come to me for whatever she needs, and I would never bat a single eyelash. She, and her family for that matter, have been there for me since I was eleven. Through *everything*. Why are you even being such a prick about this all of a sudden? You have known from day one that she is my ride-or-die. Why is this all coming up now?"

"I just. I don't know. I thought that once we were engaged. Once we get married. It should be about us. The Mike & Taylor Show. Remember? I don't want to have to share you." He dropped the garbage bag and made his way across the table to Taylor. She let down her guard when he put his arms around her shoulders.

"It's just one night, babe. It won't always be like this. She's going to get better."

"Fine. I mean, of course, babe. I'm sorry. I love you. If she's your sister then she's going to be mine too." Michael kissed Taylor on the forehead. "I just hope we can make up some time for what we were both too drunk to do last night," said Michael as he winked and slapped his fiancée playfully on the ass.

Taylor jumped with slight apprehension but then gave a giggle. "Mmmm, save it for later, Tiger. I promise we will have our own time too."

"I'ma hold you to that." Michael exclaimed as he picked up the trash bag once again, heading out the side door to the garbage bins. "Be right back. Gotta finish cleaning up this mess before she gets here. What time is she coming?"

"I don't know, honestly." Taylor checked the time on her phone. "She should have already been here by now."

Olivia sat in her car in Coffee Stop parking lot. Halfway to Taylor's house she had come to a screeching halt and whipped the car around in the opposite direction, heading to her former workplace. She wasn't 100% sure why, she just knew that explaining the murder of her fiancée's best friend, who also turned out to be a scumbag and a rapist, was not going to be an easy back and forth. Coffee Stop was the only other thing that made sense to her at the moment.

The car idled for a few minutes before the stop-start system automatically shut the engine off. More silence. It was preferable to the cavalcade of chaos she had been subjected to lately. A pair of crows on the roof of the shop broke the quiet with their raspy, rattling caws.

Olivia drifted off in a daze as she stared at the shop. The doors blurred as she lost focus. Her mind raced over every detail of the last three days, but it also rushed to knock down every image that popped into her brain and replace it with something distracting instead. A montage of recent events juxtaposed against movie clips and cartoon daydreams. Olivia's ADHD worked overtime to keep her out of a dark spiral, but it wasn't helping. In reality, it was just pushing her further down the rabbit hole but with blinders on.

Olivia shook her head and snapped out of it. Not an easy task. She was still hungover, still high, and still processing trauma. She wondered if she should go inside and explain why she left to Vividh. It seemed so silly at this point though. Everything that happened after she left made Coffee Stop feel like it was a millennia ago.

Gazing at the front of the store did bring a pang of sadness to her heart. As menial as it may have been, she did enjoy most days. She remembered the first day she applied, she remem-

bered how the whole reason she even chose this shop in particular was because it reminded her of the Quick Stop from *Clerks*,
one of her favorite films of all time. It would be fun to be the
female Dante, serving up coffee and witty banter with patrons
and coworkers, she thought. There was never much witty
banter to be had, though. Her coworkers were either too serious
or just not funny, and the customers mostly kept to themselves
unless they were the stuck-up snobby type who thought they
were entitled to the world. Olivia thought about the slain soccer
mom from her last day, opened up and hollowed out just like
her empty bottle of pills on the nightstand. A glinting beam of
sunlight reflected off the windshield and hit her in the eye as an
image of Render flashed in her mind.

THWAP!

Something hard smacked against her window and made
her damn near jump out of her moon roof.

"What the ever-loving fuck?" Olivia shouted as she turned
to see what she assumed was one of the crows suicide bombing
her driver-side window. What she saw pressed up against the
glass was even more disturbing than a splattered bird carcass.
It was the child. Chrysanthemum's creepy-eyed, cryptic quote
spewing son. He was holding both hands up and smushing
his forehead against the glass. His eyes were burning holes
through Olivia's head. She thought about how much scarier
Render would look if he had those eyes instead of those empty
sockets. She contemplated throwing the car into high gear and
hightailing it out of the parking lot. But she noticed that the boy
was crying.

"Aw, man." Olivia sighed deeply and rolled down her
window. "Uh. Hey. Little guy. What are you doing he—"

"Why did you kill my mom?" the boy screamed as he
gripped Olivia's door and leaned into the car.

"What the fu—Yo. I did not. I had nothing to do with—
Wait, what happened to your mom?" Olivia tried to play coy.

"You did it! You did it! You summoned the monster! Your
fault! I told you not to!"

Olivia grimaced and shifted uncomfortably in her seat.

The boy broke down into hysterical tears and plopped on to the curb behind him. Olivia exited the car and sat down next to him. She attempted to put her arm around the weeping child.

"Don't touch me," he yelled through spit and streams of salty tears.

"Look kid, I know what it's like to lose your parents. It's bullshit, and it's not fair, and—"

"And it's your fault," he shouted back as he wiped his eyes with a long sleeve. His face was red hot and steaming. "Why'd you have to summon that, that thing? She didn't even do anything to you. You get shitty customers all the time. My mom wasn't perfect, but you didn't have to go and get her killed! You—you… bitch!"

"Whoa! Hey. I don't know how you… know all the things that you do… but I didn't summon anything. I made one stupid vague tweet, but I didn't ask for this or call on that monster. I don't even understand why or how it came to me. I… wait a second. How *do* you know all of this? Are you a part of this stupid little game?"

"What game? My mom is dead!"

"How do I know this isn't like the world's most elaborate episode of *Scare Tactics*? Where's Tracy Morgan?"

"Who the heck is Tracy Morgan? What are you babbling about lady? All I know is what I see. I get these, like, visions all the time. I know that whatever you did, it pulled that Render guy back into our world and now he's killing people for you. Nobody ever believes me though, not my dad, not the cops…"

"You told the police about me?" Her voice was shrill with shock.

"What does it matter? I didn't give them your name. I just said some mean old lady. They thought I was just making stuff up because I was traumatized or whatever."

"I'm only thirty-four."

"What?"

"Nothing. Okay so, you're a clairvoyant? Assuming I believe

that. What else did you see? Can you tell me what that thing is or where it really came from? Or how I can get rid of it?"

"You have a black heart."

"The hell's that supposed to mean?"

"You can't even say sorry? For killing my mom?"

"I—I'm sorry. I'm so sorry."

"Save it, Olivia."

"How do you know my name?"

"Render is bound to your darkness and so are you." The boy pulled his head out from between his knees and turned toward Olivia. Those terrible eyes were suddenly gone. His face now resembled a tiny Render. Crackling static filled the air around them both. "Our bind cannot be undone, stupid girl." The boy's voice was now a synthesized, robotic growl. "And once I've fulfilled our user agreement, I'll rip away your deliciously darkened soul as well."

Olivia fell back onto her hands as she tried to scramble backward to get away from the possessed child. There was a loud sizzle and a pop before the boy's body mutated into a mass of digitized pixels and then disappeared altogether.

She splayed her hand against her chest blinking rapidly in disbelief of everything that just transpired.

"Olivia?" a second, more familiar voice called from the doorway of Coffee Stop. It was Vividh, who was furrowing his large bushy eyebrows behind his thick, black hipster glasses. He scratched the manbun on his head with a dark coffee-stained hand. Brynn must have busted the machine again. His face was plastered with concern. "You okay?"

Olivia stood up and dusted herself off. "Yeah. I'm fine. How are you?"

'How are you?' Are you kidding me Olivia?

"You sure?" Vividh continued as he took a step outside the shop and looked around before gazing back at Olivia. "Not to make it weird but, well, we've been watching you from inside the shop for like, twenty minutes. It looked like you were out here talking to yourself like a deranged homeless person."

Vividh laughed nervously.

"To myself? You didn't see that kid? He was right here."

"Kid? No, I, guess I missed him. Hey. If you need to talk to someone… I'm not mad about you leaving. Like I said the other day, I get it. You can talk to me if you need to."

"You're so sweet and I'm really sorry but I gotta go." Olivia stumbled over her words as she made her way back into her car.

"Go? You're not even coming in? Why'd you come back then?"

"Honestly? I don't know. I'm sorry." She gave him a look of sincere apology before she closed the door and attempted to escape responsibility once again.

Vividh shrugged his shoulders and stepped back inside the shop as Olivia's Camry disappeared from the parking lot.

Olivia finally arrived at Taylor and Michael's around sunset. All she wanted was to have Taylor to herself for the night, maybe to talk about what's been happening, but more-so just to talk about bullshit like they always did and find a tiny piece of normalcy amid her unraveling madness. Nonetheless, it was a hard third wheel kind of night, and Michael wasn't giving either of them an inch of room to breathe. Thus, Olivia was quiet and reserved and not at all like her usual self.

They had dinner together. Michael had gone out to pick up food from Amighetti's, a childhood favorite amongst all three of them. Olivia was so withdrawn the entire time that it was making Michael visibly uncomfortable. Olivia's cold demeanor was getting under his skin and he could barely stand it.

Taylor did her best to mediate and keep things warm and friendly but the whole night she felt like a child sitting at the table between two parents who were on the verge of a divorce. Michael rushed through dinner and used every excuse in the book to hurry himself and Taylor off to bed. Taylor could tell that Olivia's cold shoulder was now directed at her too. She had let Michael wedge himself between them, and in Olivia's eyes, that amounted to betrayal.

Olivia didn't even say goodnight as they turned in; her only utterance was a stiff, "Sleeping on the couch, right?" Taylor gave her a somber look and offered a hug, but Olivia pulled away before Taylor could reach, and then power walked away to the living room.

Soon after, Taylor brought Olivia a couple of blankets and a pillow as she prepped the living room couch for bed. Taylor dropped it all on the coffee table and squeezed her best friend as hard as she could. She didn't care if Olivia wanted to talk or not, more than anything she wanted her to feel loved and not so alone. She wanted to leave it at that, but she just couldn't help herself. She blurted out, "Okay, hon, I'm sorry, but you have to tell me what's going on. No. You literally cannot do that to me. I know something is wrong. I know something happened last night. I know you, and you know I would never judge you. If something happened with Ron, you could tell me. I know I pushed him on you pretty hard last night but he's kinda cute, right? I'm sorry. Please tell me. Please. Was it bad?"

"Oh, my God, dude. Ew. No. Stop, I just... I'm still... processing. I just, need a place to crash tonight and I need you not to ask me any questions. Okay?"

"Okay... You sure you're okay?

"No questions."

"Okay."

Olivia was sick of people asking her if she was okay. What the hell is *okay* anyway?

Taylor tried her best to leave and head back upstairs but this just wasn't normal to her. She stomped her foot and waved her body back and forth.

"Ollyyyyy! We can't just leave it like this!" she whined. Taylor's eyes darted around the room, desperate to find anything to get Olivia talking to her. Then she saw it on the coffee table, a large wooden chest shaped like a hollowed-out book.

"Okay. Can I just ask one, tiny, eensy-weensy question before I go? Please?"

"That was two questions already and... no."

Taylor completely ignored Olivia and sat on the couch-turned-bed next to her. She leaned over the table and opened the fake leather-bound book. She pulled out a large joint and a lighter as she turned to her friend with a creeping smile.

"My question is... Wanna get high?"

Olivia couldn't help it. She burst out laughing and threw her head in her hands.

Stupid! She kept her face firmly placed in her palms as she contemplated whether or not she really wanted to get high. Olivia knew where it would lead but she also yearned for a shred of something familiar. Before her life had been gutted and flipped the fuck upside down, getting stoned with her sister was her favorite pastime. She groaned and gave in, once again asking herself the dumbest question she could think of: *What's the worst that could happen?*

"Is Captain Control Freak cool with that?"

"Pssh. This is my house too. I am a grown-ass adult," she said as she held a tiny flame to the end of the long, white kush-filled cylinder. "And if I want to smoke? I'm gon—Oh shit is that him?" She flinched and crouched down after hearing a noise by the stairs.

Olivia laughed and checked to make sure the coast was clear. Taylor's cat, Mia Wallace, came bounding down the stair-case towards them.

"I think you're good. It's just Mrs. Wallace."

Taylor sat up, relieved, and took a long drag. She flippantly grabbed the TV remote and turned it on as she passed Olivia the joint

Olivia recoiled slightly as the screen came to life. Scenes from earlier in the day cycled through her brain.

"You gonna hit that *or...*?"

"Yeah. Sorry."

Olivia inhaled a dense cloud and let it sit in her throat for a moment before releasing it into the wild.

As the fog accumulated in the room and the leftover tension from dinner lifted, the duo talked and laughed about everything *except* Render or Ron or the random creepy kid that showed up at Coffee Stop. Classic cartoons played on the television, but it was more of an aesthetic filler than anything. The girls kept the volume down and carried on blazing and conversating for a little over half an hour. Taylor brought up her infamous job offer but laid off on the pressure. She simply wanted to know if Olivia was even interested in something like that.

"I mean, yeah. It's just. I don't know. Sometimes I feel stuck in my lane... Other times I feel so comfortable here and so in love with the creepypasta format that, I just don't want to take that leap into the next thing."

"I feel you; I know that you would be *great* at it if you did, but, I feel you. What attracted you to creepypastas in the first place?"

"It's the new frontier."

"Huh?"

"Like, I feel like... every myth and folklore and story that you hear had to come from someone at some point, right? Like, some person way back in time came up with all these stories, and even, like, religious beliefs and superstitions were created by some storyteller eons ago. And, I get so sick of things being rehashed and rebooted... I feel like writing these stories is a really cool way to create new, modern folklore. Urban legends that people actually start to believe in." Olivia thought about it even harder. "Maybe I will take that job though, because, what's stopping me from continuing that thought and creating new monsters? Right? Like Hollywood monsters. Our parents and the generations before them grew up with Dracula, Frankenstein, the Wolfman, the Mummy, all that. We grew up with Freddy, Jason, Leatherface, Chucky, and whatnot, and people just *keep* remaking them over and over. I want to make new monsters." Olivia liked the sound of that very much, and it was exciting for Taylor to see her friend so passionate about something for what seemed like the first time in months.

"Oh, my God, I love that! You could start with this Render creep, but, sounds like someone else already came up with all that... unless you're just fucking with me? Did you make all this up to showcase your new idea? Because I wouldn't even be mad honestly."

Olivia gave Taylor a searing-hot side-eye. She wasn't supposed to bring that up. She definitely should have known that Olivia wasn't making up shit.

"You want to see him? You really think—? I can't. I can't believe you still don't actually believe me."

"I'm sorry," Taylor nearly shouted.

"No. What the fuck, Taylor? Here." Olivia grabbed her backpack and unzipped it fervently, pulling out her phone and turning it on for the first time since she left her house, "I will fucking show you. You don't even know..."

"Whoa. Whoa. *Chill!* I believe you, Olivia, I just thought maybe..."

Olivia stopped as she thought about what was in the video. She also thought about how suspicious it was that neither Taylor nor Michael seemed even a little bit concerned about not hearing from Ron since he disappeared in the middle of the night. Olivia stared into the empty space in front of her as she played out different scenarios in her head.

She turned to Taylor. "Are—are *you* fucking with *me*?"

"I'm sorry, what?"

"Is this all a game? Am I Michael Douglas in *The Game* right now??"

"*The Game*? You're talking about the old dad from the Ant-Man movies, right?"

"Yes, dude. I fucking watched it *with you* back in the day. Remember the one where all this crazy shit happens to him, but in the end, it turns out it was all this elaborate game, and no one actually got killed and—"

"*Oh, yeah!*" Taylor stifled a laugh because she could tell that

Olivia was 100% serious. "Well, if that's what all of this is… I ain't privy to the party, my princess."

Fathoming her best friend working against her was a near impossible pill to swallow. Still, Olivia envisioned Taylor and Michael and Ron all sitting around a table, conspiring. Her jaw clenched at the thought.

"That's exactly the kind of thing you would say if you were in on it. What is it? Some sort of new, in-depth augmented reality game developed by your company? It would be pretty fucked up to pull that on someone that's currently suffering from mental trauma, Taylor."

"Olivia! Hon. I would *never* put you through something like that. And honestly, I'm a little offended that you think I'd be capable of going that low." Her tone was sharp and bitter.

Olivia didn't even notice she was crying until she felt the cold tickle of her tears rolling over her cheeks.

"Well, then what is it? Why is it happening to me? And what do I have to do to stop it?" she begged.

"Oh, sweetheart. I think, maybe if you just ignore this weirdo. Just block and—"

"No, you don't get it. I can't. And… and… there's something I have to tell you…"

"Are you guys seriously smoking *inside* the fucking house?" Michael's angry voice echoed against the interior of their foyer as he yelled from upstairs.

"*No…*" Taylor shouted back unconvincingly.

"Come on, Taylor," Michael shouted in the most disappointed dad-tone the two had ever heard.

"Tell me in the morning?" Taylor pleaded as she got up and started to walk backwards toward the stairs. "I promise, I will be here for whatever it is, and I won't judge."

Why can't I just tell you now? Olivia thought. *Are you really that much of an obedient dog to him? What happened to you, girl?*

Olivia wiped her face with the sleeve of her shirt and nodded. "Okay."

"I love you."

"Love you too."

"*Taylor?*" Michael shouted again.

"Babe! I'm coming! Jesus, Mary, and Joseph."

Taylor gave Olivia one last look as she reached the bottom of the stairs.

"Go," Olivia said with half a smile.

Taylor blew her a kiss and went to her fiancée.

"Goodnight, Taylor."

Get fucked, Michael.

Her cell phone buzzed quietly inside her backpack. Olivia was too tired and wary to see what it was. She watched the cartoon cat on the television chase a cartoon mouse, both wielding cartoon axes and taking turns at trying to slice the other open. The buzzing continued, but Olivia continued to ignore it. Slowly, the buzzing grew into a low rumble. Something next to her rattled violently. She looked to her side and noticed that she was no longer alone on the couch.

Alejandro sat next to her. He looked better this time, not like a disfigured zombie at all. It was the handsome face she remembered, with his long, straight black hair, and his skin was tan again, not discolored like a corpse. Though, she noticed he was sweating profusely, and his entire body shook and jolted. Olivia looked down and saw that in place of the couch, Alejandro was in an airline seat that was being jostled about as he looked lovingly at his sister.

"H-h-hey, midget." His voice and his entire apparition shook but his perfect smile was like a warm hug. "G-g-got a sec?"

THIRTEEN

OLIVIA GAZED AT HER BROTHER from somewhere between heartbreak and elation. "You have to stop showing up when I'm high. You're really not helping to combat my 'Holy Hell I have completely lost my God forsaken mind at this point' theory."

"You're not crazy. Deep down, you know this is all real. *All* of it." Alejandro's airplane seat was still there but the turbulence had ceased. There was a faint sound of a large fan, and Olivia wasn't sure if it was from Alejandro's phantom plane cabin or Taylor's air conditioning unit.

"No, I don't! I'm stoned as fuck right now, Alejandro! I'm probably—I *am* just imagining this. I'm imagining that my dead brother is here to talk me down because that's what my subconscious wants and, I am just, too high. Again."

"That's not how this works, Liv."

"Ew. Don't call me that. You know I hate it when you call me that." Olivia looked at her ghost of a brother then turned back to silent cartoon violence on the television, half-watching, half-staring into nothing. "I know that I hate being called that, which means my subconscious did it because I secretly hate myself and I wanted to..."

"For someone whose favorite movie used to be *Empire Records* and had a Liv Tyler poster in her room, you sure do hate to be referred to as such."

"She *was* my favorite actress. I mean like, in the 90s, yeah. I loved her, but, I never wanted to *be* her. Everyone in middle school started calling me Liv when she was blowing up and it just bothered me. I didn't want her identity; I wanted my own. I wanted to be Olly, the half Cuban half white girl, who was cute but a little creepy and borderline goth but dressed and talked like a B-girl from the Bronx."

"We've never even been to New York."

"I know. I just always felt like we were raised in that culture. You and your whole crew just exuded that vibe, and you guys always brought me along, plus, you brought me up on Wu-Tang and that grimy east coast—Why am I still conversating like this is normal? I'm either crazy, or too gone, and you're dead."

"I am definitely dead."

"That much we know."

The pair of siblings laughed, like they were kids again.

Olivia looked her brother in the eyes. "Okay, let's pretend I'm not nuts. Not too stoned for my own good."

"Well, that *is* part of it."

"So, you admit it?"

"No. Sort of. It's complicated."

"Are you about to disappear and leave me hanging? Because lately, every single time someone tells me how complicated something is and seems like they're about to unravel the truth and tell me everything I've been waiting to hear, they start glitching in front of me or throwing up or they just disappear, and it's really, really, freaking annoying."

"Luckily, you're just inebriated enough for me to get through to you with a pretty strong connection right now."

"Okay so, the weed boosted my supernatural Wi-Fi signal?

That's good. Good to know."

"Well, in a manner of speaking, yes."

"Great."

"When we are in our bodies, on Earth, there are certain frequencies that we can't tap into. The spirit world is all around us, but we can't see it because it's behind the veil. When you take something that alters your state of consciousness it opens your perception and sort of lets you peek behind that veil. See, hear, feel things you wouldn't be able to normally. Of course, to do this, it also has to shut down something else, like common sense or your inhibitions... sometimes motor functions if you've taken too much of something hard."

A memory flashed through Olivia's brain. "Like that time you had to babysit me because I ate a tad too many mushrooms and couldn't move from your floor?"

"Exactly! Do you remember the 'space gnats' you kept going on about?"

"Oh, my God, I do! I thought I could see the fabric of existence itself." Olivia laughed at how stupid it felt to say out loud.

"You could though. You did."

"Wait, what?"

"Olivia, those 'space gnats,' the stars that people see when they smack their head or stand up too fast—those things are literally *everywhere*. I'm no angel; I couldn't tell you what they're called or what they do... but it was the first thing I noticed when I arrived on the other side. Olly was right."

"*Weird*. But, again, I just feel like this is all confirmation bias by my own ego conflating my ideas and memories and creating a grand illusion for myself because I really, finally broke myself."

"Olivia," Alejandro let out a chuckle, "You're only saying all that to convince yourself. Deep down, you know just how real all of this is."

"But—"

"I need you to trust my words. The same way you always have."

"So. I'm not Michael Douglas? You're real? The cyber-demon is real... *and*, I'm an accomplice to the murder of my best friend's fiancée's best friend? Among others... Why? Why me? Why is any of this happening? Because of a fucking *tweet*? If this is some real supernatural shit, why can't God just take me out instead? Stop messing with my head... and, and *my life*, Take *me*, not these helpless people... Then at least I could be with you, and Mom and Dad again." Olivia noticed the tears rolling down Alejandro's cheeks. "I'm sorry, it's just, a lot. I can't remember the last time I saw you cry Ally. I didn't even know ghosts could cry; never really thought about it I guess..."

"Olly... Michael Douglas? Look, you have to stop doing what you're doing. You're only making it stronger."

"I'm sorry. I don't know how to not freak out about this, though. How am I supposed to process, any of this?"

"I'm not talking about how you're reacting. I'm talking about what you keep doing with your hands. You're doing it right now."

Olivia looked down at her left hand. She had been dragging her finger back and forth across the fabric of the couch without really thinking about it.

"My hands? What, that's just a nervous tick. I've always done that. I don't know what to do with my hands when my mind is racing. Does it bother you?"

"No, Olly." Alejandro stared into her eyes intently. "You really don't know what you're doing?"

Olivia returned a bewildered shrug.

"Idle hands really are the Devil's workshop..."

"Please make sense. You're scaring me."

"Olly, every time you do that when you're high, you start etching out runes and symbols and sigils. How—how do you not know that?"

Olivia looked at the impression she had made in the couch, it almost looked like a crooked game of hangman.

"What the fuck?" Olivia blurted out. "Every time? I—I didn't—Not on purpose!" She couldn't even articulate the words she was trying to say.

"You did it with a rock on the sidewalk outside of Coffee Stop the other day. You did it with a pen on your desk while you watched the Render video. You even do it in the air sometimes in the car... That's why your bond is so strong. You keep protecting him. You've been doing it so often, I guess I thought you knew. You really gotta stop smoking, sis."

"But then, I won't be able to see you?"

"Sis, you're not even *supposed* to be seeing me."

"Okay but how often are you watching me? Like, a little creeped out."

"That is not the part that should be creeping you out right now! And we don't watch you. Everything is happening at once; time and space aren't really a thing on this side... It's just kind of, there." Alejandro looked around the room and over his shoulder. There was a sudden *DING* of a fasten seat belt sign directly above his head. "I have to go, Olly."

"What? No! I still have *so* many questions! Why am I tracing sigils subconsciously? Why is this demon motherfucker a cyber-demon? Why can't I see you without drugs? What—"

"I don't have the answers you seek."

"What? Yes, you do! You're like the guardian angel of exposition all of a sudden! Come on, Ally! Don't leave me again." Olivia's voice whimpered and Alejandro's apparition began shaking and jostling about again.

"All I can tell you, is—" his words were fragmented and stilted as he fought against the unearthly turbulence. "Look into Jay Rendegger—unh!" He grunted as his body jerked forward violently. "The MalAttack-ack hoax guy— one who didn't— Ah! The one that survived! Sanct S-s-s-sariel brother—"

The sound of a roaring jet engine swallowed Alejandro's head whole and then ripped its way out of existence. Olivia covered her face. When she brought herself back up, Alejandro was gone. She was alone on the couch with an eerie silence and two dancing, muted cartoon animals. The cat and the mouse had since turned each other into ghosts with hollow eyes and squiggly little ghost tails.

Olivia was starting to feel like a cartoon herself. Jumping from one ridiculous scenario to the next. Narrowly escaping certain death. Taking emotional lump after lump and then trying to act like maybe nothing happened the next instance. She took note that she was stoned and making flimsy rationalizations but how else was she supposed to process everything she had been through? It's not every day that you find out that you've been inadvertently summoning evil spirits out of cyber space and that the afterlife is a definitively real thing. Guilt weighed down on her chest like an anvil. It had her sinking deep into the couch. Fear of what might come next made her throat feel like it was swelling shut.

Her phone buzzed again from inside her backpack. She pulled it out apprehensively. She wasn't sure how much more paranormal terror she could stomach tonight, and one more message from Render might just send her directly over the edge. She glanced at it quickly out of the corner of her eye and was instantly relieved to see Taylor's name popping up instead.

She checked the text: "Hey, are you on the phone with someone? We can hear you talking super loud from up here."

"Can you just try to keep it down a bit? Michael freaks out when he can't get to sleep."

"Plz?"

FOURTEEN

ZzzzZZZZZZzzZZZ...   ZWHIP   ZWHUMP   ZWHIP
ZWHUMP

Oh no. Please, not right now. Please.

Olivia didn't want to open up her eyes. She could feel the warmth of the morning sun surrounding her, so she at least knew she made it through the night alive. But if Render was making another surprise appearance, she just wasn't ready to face it. The maddening noise of buzzing combined with loud thumping made her fear the worst. She cracked open one eye and peered toward the direction of the commotion. Immediately her stress was alleviated and replaced by utter annoyance when she saw Michael in a tank top two sizes too small, running on the treadmill in the corner of the living room.

Really? You couldn't just wait? Or wake me up first and give me a heads up? Just — ugh.

Olivia sat up and rubbed the sleep out of her eyes, mustering a very groggy, "Morning, Mike."

"Oh, hey Olivia. You're up. Hope that's not my fault. Tried

to keep this baby on a low speed so it wasn't too loud."

"No, no. You're good," Olivia lied, "I always get up around this time." She looked at the time on her phone: 6:30AM. Olivia rarely woke up on her own before 9

On her phone was another text from Taylor, received around thirty minutes prior: "Morning Love! Had to run to the office and I didn't want to wake you up too early."

Good thing your fiancé is of the same mind, she snarked to herself.

The text went on: "Help yourself to whatever you want."

"Mikey will be working from home today so don't mind him. He mostly keeps to himself but if he's being a cranky dick-face just ignore him."

"Call me when you wake up, K? Love you, Smelly!"

Did she not remember that I had something important to tell her? And isn't she going to help me figure out what the fuck this demon wants? Or what it is? Or is she just trying to avoid me all together? I shouldn't have roped her into this anyways…

Olivia tossed her phone on the couch and tossed her head back, looking at what was on the television. She instantly recognized a familiar, contorted face with a giant smile and a large knife in their hand. A blonde-haired woman leaned over a dead fish on her kitchen counter with a butcher knife as her face grew into nightmarish cartoon proportions; it was the music video for "Black Hole Sun" by Soundgarden. She turned to Michael to say it was cool if he wanted to turn up the volume now that she was up, and perhaps apologize for her attitude and for keeping him awake last night. But as soon as she turned, she noticed he had headphones, blasting loud enough that she could just make out the gritty, melodic crooning of Chris Cornell. Michael pressed a few buttons on the treadmill and started sprinting while the machine rose, increasing the incline.

Olivia shook her head and gathered her belongings. She got up and mouthed the words, "Cool if I take a shower?"

Michael gave a thumbs up before looking over Olivia's head to watch the music video, where a plastic Barbie doll melted on a spit roast over the dancing flames of a charcoal grill.

In the shower, Olivia let the water run over her head while she stood hunched, still as a perched gargoyle. She became deeply pensive. She played out every scenario from the past few days in her head. She thought about everything her brother had told her and tried to piece together the parts that actually made sense. She held her hands together, doing her best to keep them from pantomiming anymore inadvertent invocations. Why the hell was she doing that in the first place?

If this thing is a demon, then it clearly wants souls, right? That's what every demon wants isn't it? Can't it just take mine? How do I offer myself instead of my enemies? Maybe if I smoke just a tiny bit, I can talk to Ally again... No. No, that's a terrible idea. No more pot for you Olivia Peramo.

Steam rose from the shower door and fogged over the glass mirror of Taylor's master bath. Olivia could have stayed under the cascading hot water for hours. It was one of the first times she had felt truly safe since the start of this psychotic, supernatural episode. As if those thirty odd square feet of tile and glass were completely removed from the rest of the material world, if only for a moment.

Sure enough, as soon as she turned off the water, the existential dread of the real world came rushing back in. Olivia thought about how her brother mentioned that time and space were not constructs of the other side, and she thought about how nice it sounded to not have those two terrible things weighing you down and constantly crushing your soul. Even before she was being stalked and made a pawn for a demonic hit list, before she lost her family and her sanity, as far back as Olivia could remember she had lived in a state of panic over time. Time, responsibility, and commitment were three of her biggest fears, and she couldn't even come up with a valid reason why. She had pills for that, but she hadn't taken her meds since losing her family. Up until now she had felt like she deserved to experience every inch of her guilt. Like she really needed to suffer. It was the least she could do for them.

I should have grabbed my meds before I ran out of the house... but then, it might have blocked my ability to see Alejandro again...

She thought about the last thing he tried to tell her before being stripped away from her again.

Shit. What did he say? What the hell was that guy's name? What did he say it was? Jay something! Jay Rendegger... Something about his brother? Ugh, I need to research this shit.

She looked at her phone as she got dressed. While she could easily use it for a quick Google search to facilitate all the research she needed, she still wasn't feeling 100% about using any technology that Render had crept his digitally demonic tendrils into. Olivia decided that the St. Louis Public Library might be her best bet.

Olivia packed up everything she had into her Jansport and went to look for Michael to let him know she would be leaving.

The home was specifically quiet, in a certain way you can only experience inside a large house or building: menacingly calm, echoes of white noise skating along the tiles and getting muzzled out by the expensive Indonesian rugs. A low discordant hum creeps around the corners of every hallway but when you actually stop to listen or try to pinpoint where it's coming from you realize its only in your head. It's like the physical embodiment of the eerie silence before a jump scare in a horror movie, lulling you into a false sense of security even though you already know something terrible is about to pop out.

She made her way to the office, where she assumed Michael would be, but instead found an empty desk chair. She was about to turn away, when her eyes were drawn to the computer screen he had left on. It was idling on a picture of herself in a small black bikini. An old picture from years ago when they had all gone to the Lake of the Ozarks for spring break. Before she could even ask herself why the hell he would be going through old pictures of her, she noticed the squirt bottle of moisturizing lotion and the box of tissues flanking the keyboard, and the pathetic wadded-up ball of tissue on the floor.

"Michael, dude. Gross," she said out loud before she could stop herself.

Just then, she heard the toilet of the office's en suite bathroom flush. She tried to whirl herself around and step as far away from the computer as she could before he came out, but he flung the door open too quickly. Michael let out a small yelp as he jumped backwards.

"Oh shit! Olivia, I'm sorry, I thought you were still in the shower." He was still wearing his miniscule tank top and gym shorts. Olivia could tell from the bulge inside of them, that he was still semi-hard. His eyes tracked her gaze and then darted over to the computer screen.

"Olivia. It's not — This is *not* what it looks like."

"You sure, Mikey? Because it looks like you were masturbating to old pictures of *me* like a super creep."

"Okay. So. It *is* what it looks like but—" He took a step toward Olivia, trying to place his hands on her shoulders, and Olivia took a step back.

"No, no, no, Mike. This is just too much for me. I'm sorry."

I'm sorry? Why the hell am I sorry??

"Olivia. You have to understand." Michael's face turned to panic as he realized that she wasn't at all into his advances and would surely be mentioning this to her best friend. "I love Taylor. Okay? I do! This is just... I just figured... and you're so..."

Fucking ew. Bullshit you love her, you love your own dick and you're not even trying to hide it.

"Mike. You are literally saying nothing right now."

"You can't tell her, Olivia. You can't!" He slammed his hand against the open bathroom door. Olivia jumped a little when she noticed how strong he was. Much stronger than his puny friend that couldn't keep it in his pants either. She had a feeling he wouldn't be as easily deterred.

Come on, Mike. Don't fucking do this.

Olivia felt a new kind of fear bubbling up inside her throat. Michael pounded the door again, this time with a closed fist. She was surprised it didn't leave a hole.

"Woah! You need to chill the fuck out *right* now and you need to not be creepy about this, Michael. I cannot tell you how poorly timed and *wildly* inappropriate this is. The list of insanity and bullshit I've had to go through lately has just been so much more than I can physically take, and this? Mike, what the fuck, man? I really thought you were one of the last good men out there. I was *so* happy for Taylor. You have a fucking problem; this is not okay." She shook her head as she looked up at the ceiling. "I am so disappointed in yo— Michael!"

When she looked back down, she saw that Michael was even more erect than before. Olivia's degradation was turning him on.

"I can't help it, okay?" Michael bolted to the door frame and blocked her only exit. "If you tell her… I'm just going to tell her *you* came on to me first. Yeah! You basically forced yourself onto me. Or… We can just pretend this never happened and you can keep pretending like you don't secretly want to rip off these shorts and see my cock for yourself."

This can't be real. Out of everything, somehow, this is the most unbelievable and it's happening right in front of me. What if I can't get away this time? I can't overpower this meathead.

Olivia's eyes welled up. She shifted her stance and gripped the shoulder straps of her backpack like it was her parachute. It was in that moment that Olivia remembered what was nestled safely inside of her backpack. A gentle breeze of relief blew into her chest. Still, her grip didn't loosen. She wasn't prepared to exhale just yet. Olivia had never actually used a gun and she was terrified that he might call her bluff. Michael slowly edged closer to her as an evil grin crept across his face. Olivia's fear mutated into rage. Michael's audacity and entitlement were flashing red lights blaring in her face. It was now or never.

Olivia gave Michael a look that could have sliced his body in twain if she let it. "Okay. This is what we're doing?" she asked Michael as she dropped the backpack from her shoulder and began zipping it open. "This is what we're doing." She continued as she pulled out her father's handgun and aimed it directly at Michael.

"Woah! What are you doing you crazy b—"

"Oh, Michael, I dare you to call me a bitch. *Please* call me a bitch right now," she threatened as she marched toward Michael, keeping the firearm firmly trained on his face.

"Please stop," he whimpered as she got close enough to press the barrel of the gun against his cheek.

"Now. I'm going to leave, Michael. I'm going to leave, and I am going to tell Taylor *everything*. You can go ahead and tell her whatever you want, and she might believe you. Or? She might believe me. Right now, I really don't give a fuck. But I have had a *bad fucking weekend* and the last thing I need right now is your frat-boy, fuck-boy, silver spoon fed, pretty prince of white privilege ass making it any worse. Do you understand me?" she asked firmly, her face nearly pressed up against his ear. "I wouldn't cross me right now, Michael. That hasn't been working out too well for folks lately. Now would you kindly get the flying fuck out of my way?" She finished in a sweet whisper

Michael stepped to the side and cowered down to the floor as Olivia stuffed the gun back into her bag and left him in a pathetic wadded-up ball on the floor.

FIFTEEN

ADRENALINE WAS ROCKETING THROUGH OLIVIA'S veins as she drove away from Taylor's house. She had never pulled a gun on anyone in her entire life. It was exhilarating and terrifying. It gave her courage to think that she could do the same to Render if given another opportunity. The thought of that confrontation raised butterflies in her throat.

Olivia sat in her car outside the Daniel Boone branch of the St. Louis Public Library. She tried to call Taylor multiple times on the drive over, but she wasn't answering. Probably busy at work. Possibly, Mike got to her first. She didn't care. Olivia was no longer in league with questioning her own truth. After everything she had seen, and everything she knew she had experienced, she knew now what was real and what was a figment of her imagination. She knew because she saw it happen right in front of her blood-soaked eyes and felt it all the way down to the raw meat beneath her skin and the marrow in her bones. The worst part about it though, was that the truth was sad, terrible, and irredeemably, utterly fucked.

Until this moment, Olivia had been seething with rage but now the tears flooded in hot. She clenched her jaw and screamed through her teeth as she dropped a hailstorm of punches on her steering wheel.

Olivia typed out a long and detailed text message to Taylor, explaining everything from the attempted rape by Ron Mitchell to his gory destruction at the hands of Render, to the sleazy sexual assault from her fiancée. She left out her brother's ghost, knowing that it would be detrimental to her credibility, especially when it was Michael's word against hers.

Sent.

Olivia tried to call one more time.

No answer.

She put the phone down and peered at the entrance of the library. It was important not to lose focus now. Given his track record, Michael would be next on Render's list, and Olivia needed to find a way to stop him before he struck again.

Olivia made her way inside and went straight up to the first person she saw at the checkout counter, a tall woman with dark hair and a kind smile.

"Excuse me, ma'am."

"Yes, how can I help you?"

"Where are the um—what do you call them? The old machines that let you scroll through old newspaper articles and—"

"Microfiche readers?"

"Yes! I mean, I think? Those are the ones you see in all the movies, right?"

"Erm, right… but, we haven't had a microfiche reader available in years."

"Oh. Shit. Sorry! Shoot. Well, what do you use now?"

"The internet, my dear." The librarian motioned towards the row of computers behind Olivia.

"Right. Of course," Olivia laughed and slowly backed away from the desk.

"The computers are free to use as long as you have a valid

library card."

"Thank you very much."

Offput by Olivia's flat tone and defeated demeanor, the librarian gave her a quizzical look as she slowly shuffled her feet toward the computer bank. "You, do have a library card?"

"Yeah. Uh, used to come here all the time. Think I have it on me…"

"Oh, you can just use your email address and access number for the pass… word." Her voice trailed off as Olivia turned away from her completely.

"Perfect."

Olivia was well aware of how to access the library computers; she had spent half of her high school career in this library. Which made her realize that she should have known better about the microfiche machines, she didn't even remember ever seeing one.

Eight computers in all, four on one side, mirrored by four more on the other with small partitions in between. They all looked ancient and slow. Three of the computers on the opposite side were in use, the four in front of Olivia were available, she took a seat at the mini cubicle on the corner.

Olivia got to work quickly. First, she perused the library's stock, searching for any books she could find on demons and paranormal entities which was dismal at best, but she wrote down the locations of the few she did find. Next, she set her sights on Google, looking up everything she could find on Jay Rendegger and Stephen Holloway. Alejandro had only mentioned the former, but she figured looking into both of their backgrounds could help cast a wider net. There wasn't much on either, however. A few *Wired* articles on the two and their team at MalAttack from before the infamous hoax video surfaced. An article about how MalAttack was going to revolutionize the antispyware game, if it really did everything they had claimed it would. Subsequent stories about how CarcosaTech were in way over their heads and overpromising results that they were never able to deliver, hence the "suicide" and the concurrent hoax video.

What the hell was that weird Latin name Ally tried to spit out before he vanished? Sanct Sara? Sara's brother? Shit. Why does he only give me valuable information when I'm too high to remember it?

Olivia tried as many combinations as possible, versions of what she thought she had heard, with little to no results. She blinked at the screen and toyed with one of the little golf pencils the library kept in abundance by each computer. Finally, a last-ditch effort of an idea popped into her brain. She typed the words: Rendegger Sanct. Before she even finished typing it out, an autocomplete suggestion appeared with the words, "Rende-gger, Sanct Sariel Brotherhood."

Olivia followed the suggested path and found a link that led her to a digital ledger of sorts, listing the last names of past and present members of what looked to be a cult called Sanct Sariel Brotherhood. The website was unremarkable. It looked like it hadn't been updated since the early 2000's. It reeked of the Geocities and Angelfire era of the internet. Plain text floating over a clip art image of the cosmos, more clip art photos in the side bar, glowing green fonts and "under construction" gifs super imposed over digital caution tape. Olivia clicked on the "ABOUT" link and was greeted by a jarring wall of text.

"...We seek to establish a universal brotherhood melding the world of the spiritual with modern science..."

It was a truly massive sprawl of pseudo-spiritual jargon that almost seemed as if it were meant to bore the reader to the point that anyone, ADHD or not, would lose interest and turn away.

What is this? A test of my will? Olivia scrolled through, letting her eyes wander and skip around until a standout word or phrase caught her eye.

"...We beseech the Gods for their guidance and their protection and through our undying devotion and servitude we are granted with their highest blessings... ...offerings of alchemical teachings and studies... ...for a small monthly fee, we offer guidance, higher learning, and spiritual protection... ...armor yourself in the rapture of the ethereal..."

Olivia finally got to the bottom of the page and found an almost unnoticeable link at the very end, a single capital letter R, underlined in signature blue hyperlink color, camouflaged into the blueish, purple background of the page. Clicking through brought her to another underdeveloped webpage with an eye-gouging, black and white houndstooth background. In the center of the page was a monochrome image of an ancient-looking woodcut, depicting a cloaked figure with an awfully familiar face. An unnaturally large and impossibly toothy smile stretched across its lower half. The nose and eyes had been removed, and in their place were hollow sockets with tattered gory edges. It was Render from a bygone era, only now his hair was long and wild and instead of his crisp pinstriped suit, the figure was adorned in a dark hooded robe. Olivia noted that his black leather gloves were missing as well, but the hands were marginally darker than the skin depicted on his wretched face, as if the hands beneath the gloves were black as soot themselves. The figure's right hand was holding a long and very thin dagger. The left hand was outstretched and open-palmed with a menacing black spider resting in it. Beneath the hooded demon was a name inscribed in letters that resembled alphabetic runes; RONOMALIUS.

"Ronomalius?" Olivia whispered to herself out loud. "Is that your real name?" She whispered it again just to hear it once more. After saying the name Render so many times, it didn't sound right, but the image, that face, was undeniable. She tried to print a copy of the image as well as a copy of the cult's ledger, but as soon as the prompt for printing preferences showed up, the computer screen started to glitch.

"No, no, no-no-no!"

"*Shhhh*!" the librarian from the front desk shushed and gave Olivia a stern look.

"Sorry," she mouthed quietly and turned back to the computer.

A new window popped up on its own, another webcam show. The picture was blurred and grainy, but Olivia instantly recognized the walls of Mike's office., The screen glitched once more and then came into focus.

Olivia let out a quick, shrill scream and threw her hands over her mouth. There was no show to be had this time. Whatever happened had already transpired. Instead, there was a still image of Mike in his office chair, still wearing his two-sizes-too-small tank top, now dripping red with blood.

His eyes were open wide, staring off into nothing, his mouth open but empty. Beneath his chin, a large gash stretched from behind one ear to the other, and hanging down from the open wound was Mike's tongue, like an impromptu necktie. Olivia stared in horror for a moment before trying to violently click the X on the window to no avail. The screen was frozen on Mike's mutilated corpse. Olivia slammed the mouse against the desk and screamed "Just *stop!*" louder than she meant to.

All four of the users on the other side of the computer bank looked up from their screens. Olivia looked up from hers and jumped out of her seat when she saw that all four of the people had Render's face. The one closest to her slowly rose from their seat and edged towards her, its face rotating and glitching as it moved

Olivia screamed again and a firm hand in a leather glove came down on her shoulder. She whipped around and held up the golf pencil, ready to stab it into Render's decrepit face. She stopped only inches from her assailant when she realized the leather hand on her shoulder belonged to Theresa, the girl she met at Taylor and Michael's engagement party.

Theresa was in full riding gear and holding a motorcycle helmet in her other hand. She must have just rode in for her shift. Olivia had completely forgotten her mentioning that she worked here. Theresa put up her hand to dodge Olivia's attack. "Woah! You okay, sister??"

Olivia took a few steps back muttering, "Sorry" over and over, completely bewildered.

She turned to look back at the army of Renders that had spawned at the computer bank. Gone. All four of their faces had reverted to regular, albeit genuinely concerned, human faces. Panic set in as Olivia remembered the frozen image of Michael's desecrated corpse on the computer, but that too was gone. The computer had reset to its normal landing page.

"But it was — They were — "

"Tina?" Theresa spoke to the woman behind the counter. "I know I'm late for my shift, but I need to take a quick moment with my friend here."

The other librarian looked over the rim of her glasses at Olivia then back at Theresa. "Theresa, you're ten minutes early and I've never seen you take a break once. Not to mention your friend is causing quite the distraction. *Please,* take her outside."

Outside the building, Olivia and Theresa sat against the red brick exterior and talked for a long time. Theresa smoked Newports, and every pull she took made Olivia yearn for a hit of weed. She did her best to keep her urges contained.

Olivia wasn't sure why she felt so much trust in Theresa. They had only met the other night; they had only talked for so long and yet there was something about her that Olivia instantly gelled with. It felt like they had been friends already, and for quite some time. There was unspoken trust and familiarity between them, and it was for that reason that Olivia broke down and divulged everything to Theresa; every single detail about her issues with demons, murder, guns, ghosts and marijuana. It all came spilling out of her being. If the average spilling of guts was considered word vomit, this was word food poisoning. It hurt something terrible, but she couldn't stop it if she tried.

Theresa didn't skip a beat. Every word Olivia spoke to her rang true. The implicit underlying trust was a mutual thing. She knew the sincerity in Olivia's voice and in her eyes. As insane as it all was, she had no reason not to trust Olivia's story. Her eyes welled up with tears when Olivia got to Mike's unfortunate antics. She gasped when they got to the final revelation of his fate. Mike was a pig, that was certain. It hurt to think that someone she had spent so many years befriending could turn out to be another wolf wearing sheep skin. She knew he could be cunning, conniving even—it was why he went to law school—but that was a low she never expected from him.

"What would you do?" Olivia's eyes were bloodshot and not from her favorite past time.

"Well." Theresa thought hard and chose her words carefully, seeing that Olivia was in a fragile state. "I think, I would call Taylor again. To be honest. Maybe, like, don't admit anything outright, kind of like test the waters first and gauge her reaction? You said it was a still image of Mike on the computer in there, right? What if Render was just messing with you? What if he manipulated an image to try and break you and—"

"*Yo!* Is that Olivia Peramo? No freaking way, dude!" The call came from across the parking lot. Abrupt and alarming like a cop shouting at you from the megaphone in their car.

"No. Freaking. Way."

Theresa and Olivia both looked up to see a young woman in a large, unzipped hoodie, a D.A.R.E. tee turned crop top and plaid pajama pants walking toward them. Her hair was black with streaks of blue jutting out from beneath a bright red beanie that matched the red headphones dangling around her neck.

Nicky Kaughman. Her older brother Rob had always been one of Alejandro's closest friends, and even though she was always a grade younger than Olivia, she would make it a point to tagalong as often as she could. Rob was the neighborhood weed man and a stereotypical stoner. Nicky clearly followed every one of his footsteps. Their family came from the West Coast and from the way she talked to the way she slung her hat backwards and slightly to the side, it showed.

Nicky waved as she stepped closer. "Bro, I haven't seen you in hella years! How you been? Still writin' scary stories and shit?"

Olivia answered hesitantly, wishing for the solitude she had been enjoying with Theresa. "Nicky! Um, yeah. Are you still..."

"Selling weed? Ha! You know it."

"Wow okay, heh. Good to see you. Um, Nicky, this is Theresa. Theresa, Nicky Kaughman."

"Sup."

"Hi. Actually, you look crazy familiar..." Theresa squinted as she spoke. "Did you ever slang outside of Lafayette High?"

"Um, probably?" Nicky thought hard and laughed at herself. "Lafayette sounds mad familiar."

"Right." Olivia had been irritated before Nicky even joined their company. Now she was setting imaginary fire to the interloper's feet inside her mind. "Look, Nicky, it's great to see you but right now —"

"You guys want to blaze?"

A frisson of excitement flashed across Theresa's face, subsequently replaced by dejection. "I can't. I have to start my shift in like..." She checked her watch. "Five minutes ago. But you guys can. I don't mind."

"Do you need to go, Theresa? I'll be okay," said Olivia.

"No. Tina will understand. I'm going to stick around for a bit." The two exchanged reassuring smiles and a warm feeling of acceptance

Nicky held out the joint she had already lit and taken a hefty drag from. Olivia eyed the jazz cigarette with disdain, disquiet, and desire. She was far past the internal monologuing and arguing with herself about whether she should or should not partake. At this point it was obvious that she wouldn't be able to refrain if she had a hundred fucks left to give. She grabbed the jay and took a long pull.

The three sat in their circle of smoke making awkward small talk until the reefer was but a roach. Nicky offered one last puff to Olivia, but she declined. Nicky shrugged her shoulders and popped what was left of it into her mouth, embers and all. She winced, gulped, and swallowed it whole. She grinned like an idiot as the last legs of smoke spiraled out of her maw. Olivia and Theresa leaned away from Nicky giving her a strong serving of side-eye.

Nicky coughed and wheezed. "What?"

"Why the hell did you eat the roach, Nicky?"

"*Uh*... because it gets you like ten times higher? Duh?"

"Nicky."

"What? Your brother is the one who showed me that shit back in the day. Or was it my brother?"

"Oh, Nicky, no. No, no, no. They were playing with you, girl. They tried to tell me and Taylor the same shit... Have you been eating roaches for—when did we graduate? '05? You've been eating roaches for 15 years, Nicky?"

"Pssh... No. I mean, not all the time." She shuffled her feet. Nicky had indeed swallowed every single roach she had smoked since 2005. "Hey! You guys hear about the St. Louis Slasher?"

Olivia and Theresa exchanged nervous glances and lied simultaneously. "No."

"Yeah, man. Some dude stabbed the shit out of this lady in St. Charles with a switch blade. Yeah. Sick shit, right? Get this. Next day, he got the lady's kid too."

Olivia's heart sank to her stomach.

"Yup. Some people are straight fucked in the head. I mean, I thought about stabbing a broad or two, but I wouldn't actually do that shit. Unless they came at me first, y'know? And taking out a kid? Gotta be cold as a witch's titty in a Kansas City winter to stab a kid, man."

Olivia had a feeling her encounter with the child was of an otherworldly presence, but she thought she was hallucinating at the time. She hadn't even fathomed that Render would go after a kid. And for what?

"Well. It's been real, ladies, but I got some business to conduct."

"In the library, Nicky?"

"Yeah, dude! Free Wi-Fi and the cops can't trace shit back to my computer." said Nicky as she stuck out her tongue.

"Don't you use your library card to login, though?" asked Theresa.

"Yeah, my mom's."

Olivia gave Theresa a look that said don't bother. They said their goodbyes and Nicky waltzed into the library smelling and looking like a Cypress Hill concert.

Theresa asked Olivia if she was okay. Olivia assured her she was. Theresa asked again. She wanted to ask before Nicky barged her way into their space. She wanted to ask the night of Mike and Taylor's party. She could read it all over Olivia's face. Olivia had been going through a hell of a lot. Theresa stood up and gave Olivia a bear hug. She knew it was beyond overdue. Olivia didn't even fight it. She melted into Theresa and cried again. She stayed there for a long time.

When they finally broke Olivia had a revelation. "I have to go to the cops. Turn myself in."

It was the only logical thing to do. The ethical thing. Blood was on her hands. A child was dead. One way or another, the trail of bodies would lead back to her. If she was going to put a stop to this, she needed to be held accountable.

Theresa was hesitant to agree. She didn't believe that Olivia was at fault, this was something beyond her conscious control. Bigger forces were at work here. Still, she could tell that Olivia had her mind set on this and who was she to try and stop her? Even if it meant losing a newfound friend.

Olivia stared out at the parking lot then turned her gaze to the sky. She took in the immense gray clouds that shrouded the crest of the tree line and drank it down like it was the last sky she might see for a long time.

Theresa took in Olivia one last time in case it was the last time she would be seeing her. From her long wavy black hair that matched her baggy black, hooded cardigan perfectly, to the scuffed black and white Chuck Taylor's that complimented her shapely acid-washed blue jean wrapped legs, Theresa noticed Olivia fidgeting awkwardly with her fingers as she dazed. She wanted to keep reassuring her. She grabbed the twitching hand and held it tight.

"You're going to be okay." She looked her dead in the eye.

Olivia pulled her hand away and held it in front of her own face. "I—"

"I'll be off in a few hours. How about I take you in then? It'll give you some time to think it over too."

Olivia folded her hands together slowly and nodded. Theresa gave her one last look and returned to the library. Before Olivia could say another word, she was already inside the building. As Olivia made her way back to her car, her leg started buzzing and vibrating. She ripped her cell phone out of her pocket and looked at the caller ID: Incoming video call from "Taytay".

Taylor!

Olivia brushed a strand of hair behind her ear and answered the call. Taylor's face popped into the screen, her blonde curly hair filling out the frame. It was clear she had been crying, her eyelids pink and drooping, the eyes behind them defeated and bone tired.

"Taylor. Taylor, I can explain everything!"

Taylor let out a soft whimper, and tears rolled out of her swollen eyes.

"Why… why me… Olly?" said Taylor in the weakest of whispers.

"Taylor, it's not you, and nothing happened between us, but you have to know… do you… already know?"

Taylor rolled her eyes. Upwards at first, then all the way back in her head. Slowly, the camera moved backwards revealing the entire picture.

"Taylor?"

Taylor was not the one holding the phone. Taylor was on her knees with her arms obscured behind her back in the middle of an empty yellow hallway. Beige carpeting stretched beneath her, devoid of any patterns, designs, or descriptors, aside from the burgundy pool of blood that she was kneeling in. Her stomach was covered in stab wounds, her once grey camisole was now slick with the sheen of dark, sticky blood. Her body convulsed. Olivia shrieked at a volume she had never heard her voice reach before. The camera on Taylor's phone shook as someone placed it down. Render stepped into view.

Olivia…

Render craned his neck to smile at the camera. He cantered over toward Taylor's bleeding torso. As he moved, he rapidly opened and closed the stiletto blade of his switchblade knife. The popping sound of the knife made Olivia's chills dive deeper and deeper with each press of the switch. He rounded on Taylor and grabbed her by the chin with his gloved hand, pressing his thumb and forefinger into the sides of her lips. Render spread her mouth into a gruesome smile. Just like his.

"Stop!" Olivia screamed. "Come and get me instead, you gangly motherfucker! Why the hell do you keep doing this? I didn't ask for this! I love her… you malfunctioning, fucking, demonic …shit-widget!" She dragged her hand down her face. Her brain scrambled. Then, it clicked. "Ronomalius! That is your fucking name, isn't it?"

The cyber-demon became rigidly still.

Olivia watched the demon.

"Yeah, motherfucker! Ro-no-malius! Ronomalius, I command you to stop and crawl back inside of your own cyber-satanic asshole!"

Render tilted his head to the side as a cold synthetic voice with a metallic edge, devoid of humanity, came forth from behind his clenched white teeth. The sound of static surged through the phone's speaker as he spoke.

"Command not found." Each word stilted, spoken in slow angular slivers. "Our user agreement has not yet ended, Olivia Peramo. We are bound by code and by blood. You and you alone possess the key that summoned me from the confines of cyber-netic ether. Thanks to you and the… task, you've assigned, I am brimming with efficacy." He flexed his head backwards and inhaled a sharp, rattling breath. "Do not fear. I will come for you next. Your blood and your soul will be the most gratifying to spill. Any chance… of banishing me… will die with you."

"Come for me now, you fucking coward! You don't need

her! Take me!" Olivia wasn't demanding anymore, she was begging.

"In time."

Render's head flipped side to side frenziedly, then snapped back into place, locking his face on the screen as he pressed it to the side of Taylor's. His gloved hand rose, clutching his slender switchblade. He pressed the handle against the nape of her neck. *Pop.*

It opened one last time. Slicing into her throat. Exploding out of the other side. Blood cascaded from her neck and mouth. Something or someone let out a garbled and guttural, mechanical scream like an ancient dial tone being shredded through an amplifier.

The screen became pixelated and fragmented. The noise rose to a screeching crescendo. The call ended. Olivia screamed at the sky. As hard as she could. Her phone slid out of her shaking hand and crashed against the concrete.

SIXTEEN

Wish I knew what you were lookin' for/
Might have known what you would find…
-The Church "Under the Milky Way"

THERESA STRUGGLED TO MAKE IT through her shift. The snug silence inside the library was driving her insane. Aside from the soft shuffle of shoes against the braided carpet from in between the stacks and the occasional muffled clunk of books being placed back on the shelf, the library was an anechoic chamber. Every once in a while, Theresa caught the distinct raspy, nasal tones of Ghostface Killah's voice over the whispering hisses of hi-hat crashes emanating from Nicky's headphones by the computer bank. It did little to save her from the eerie quiet and the apathetic crawling of the hands on the clock.

She thought about Olivia and what turning herself in to the cops would mean. Thinking about the implications of Render made goosebumps run across her arms and down her back. She decided to try to convince Olivia not to do it. Offering her a helping hand she sorely needed seemed to be the best option. That was it. She thought about texting Olivia, but she would wait to call her until her shift ended, which felt like an eternity away.

Theresa passed the remaining time by thumbing through her own copy of VALIS by Philip K. Dick. Surrounded by dim lighting, the gray carpet looked purple. Beige countertops and endcaps burned orange. Thoughts of Halloween drifted through the weeping willows in her mind as she looked around, hardly able to pay attention to anything she read. Ennuied, she returned to her book until a commotion arose from the printer near the computer bank.

"The hell, man?" Nicky's twang rose above the hushed room. "Yo, can I like, get a hand over here? Your printer aint doin' a damn thing right."

Theresa jogged as quickly and softly as sonically possible toward the disgruntled woman, who was clearly seconds away from slapping the machine into submission.

"Hey girl, what seems to be the problem?" she whispered.

"I'm just trying to print out some directions, but your antique machinery here doesn't want to cooperate. Feel me?"

"Print out directions? Like, maptrack.com directions?"

"Duh."

"Couldn't you just use the GPS on your phone, Nicky?"

"What are you a cop? I'm not about to give up my location to Skynet when I'm tryin' to move weight, dummy. Can you help me out here or not??"

"Um. Yeah. Sometimes it just takes a little —" Theresa shook her head and cleared the error code on the printer. She stood back as it resumed its last printing job. The machine hummed and droned as the tiny pins struck against the ink ribbon. "Looks like there was an unfinished print job ahead of you. Though…" she looked around at their next-to-empty surroundings. "They probably left without it."

Nicky wasn't paying attention. She was deep in a new text conversation on her phone.

Theresa looked at the paper emerging form the printer. It

was taking up a fair amount of ink. Once the paper was a little more than a quarter of its way out, she pieced together a morbid picture. This must have been the image Olivia was describing at the tail end of her story. The one she came to the library to find: a picture of Render's true form.

It finished printing and Theresa tore it away from the printing tray before Nicky could catch a glimpse. Her directions printed immediately after.

"There you go. Should work fine now."

"*Word*. Thanks ma. Appreciate ya."

Theresa nodded and hurried back to her desk, her eyes poring over the image of Render. Ronomalius. She uttered the name to herself under her breath and studied every minute detail of the cryptic woodcut. As she repeated the name again in an almost inaudible whisper, she heard a disturbance outside followed shortly by a bloodcurdling scream.

Theresa looked around to see if anyone else besides her had heard the same thing, but not even Nicky gave so much as a hint of awareness. She wondered whether or not she had imagined the sound. She looked back at the paper, then back to the clock. One more hour to go.

She took a picture of the printout with her phone and sent a copy to Hector, asking if he had any insight on the insidious suspect. One last gander and she folded up the printed image and shoved it in her back pocket.

Head in her hands, she pretended to read her book. She found herself lost in her thoughts about demons, apparitions, dreams, and liminal spaces, the words on the page becoming a blur. Theresa's mind wandered through the impetuous and harrowing odyssey of Olivia Peramo. That girl sure was a whole lot of trouble. Troubled past. Troubled mind. Troubled waters that she was currently drowning in. That was okay with Theresa; her mother always said she went looking for trouble. The truth was that trouble had its way of finding her.

SEVENTEEN

OLIVIA HAD NO IDEA HOW long she had been sitting in her car. The cobalt blue sky and deep lilac clouds with neon orange outlines let her know that the sun was almost done setting. Resting her head against the window, buried in her hoodie, she stared into an abyss that she was well aware was staring back at her. Her right hand was heavy. Her eyes were dry. She wasn't sure she had any tears left inside her. She was numb. She didn't flinch, almost didn't even notice when Theresa rapped on the passenger window. Olivia rolled the window down without even looking to acknowledge who or what she was potentially letting in.

"*Hey*. Sorry, I tried to call a few times, but it went straight to voicemail." Theresa's brow was furrowed with concern. "Have you been waiting here this whole time? You could have come inside and—Yeah. Sorry. Probably wanted some time to yourself. Listen to your own playlist and whatnot?"

Olivia hadn't even realized until just then that "Cuts You Up" by Peter Murphy was blaring out of her car stereo. She turned the volume down and finally looked at Theresa with beggared eyes.

"Can — can I come in?"

Olivia didn't speak but unlocked the doors. Theresa placed her helmet on the seat of her motorcycle, which she had conveniently parked directly next to Olivia's car. She got in the passenger seat and folded her hands on her lap.

"How you doin'?" Theresa waited for a response. Wading in dead air. "That good huh? …You still want to turn yourself in?"

"No."

"Oh?"

"Nah. That bastard got Taylor — "

"*What?*"

" — and I know what to do now. How to really end this."

"Olivia."

"You don't have to stay here, Theresa. I appreciate you. I do. But you don't need to get yourself dragged into my Hell too. You've already circled the perimeter. If you get pulled into this, you'll just get torn apart like the rest of them."

"I'm sure as shit not afraid of this boogeyman, and think I'm tough enough to survive you, Olivia."

Olivia slowly turned her head toward Theresa.

Well, that's good. 'Cause I'm not. She wanted to say it with her chest. She said it with her eyes instead and didn't utter a word.

Olivia's right hand tensed around the handle of her father's handgun as it hung by her legs. She imagined herself pulling it out. Pressing it up against that soft spot under the chin. Right behind the lower jaw. Giving the inside of the car a new paint job. Tiny pink chunks of brain dangling from Theresa's short spritely hair. Shards of Olivia's skull shrapnel stabbing into the headliner. Both jaws gaping open, Theresa's in horror, Olivia's in pieces. She thought about who would have to clean up another one of her messes. Physically and emotionally. The stain left by Olivia Peramo, an ever-spreading cancerous mold spore. Infecting anything it touches, even after death.

"Olivia," Theresa bit the inside of her lips for a second and took a deep breath, "I can clearly see that adorable little hand cannon hanging next your legs. And girl, unless you're planning on loading that thing with a silver bullet and pulling it on that computerized Freddy Krueger when he finally shows up, I suggest you disarm yourself right now. Or I will. My mother is a cop, father is an ex-marine. I am on your side, but if I see that you have become a threat to yourself? I will not hesitate to flex on you, my love. My friend. I'm sorry, just, please put the gun down."

Olivia locked eyes with Theresa. Her eyelids were burning the same way they burned after pulling an all-nighter. Begging for sleep but pushing through the raging dawn. The Ruger was practically dripping with sweat from her palm.

Olivia broke her stare and looked into the rear view. She wasn't at all surprised to see Alejandro sitting stoically in the back seat. At least this time he looked like an actual ghost. A translucent, white, mist in the shape of her late great brother. He had no words for her. He only shook his head. She knew everything he wanted to tell her. The gun dropped with a thud.

Olivia wiped her hands on her pants and let out a gusty breath she didn't know she had been holding. "Sorry."

"Don't be."

"He's really taken everything from me now. Everything I touch will die by his hand. So, if I can't kill myself... then maybe I should just sit here and wait for him to kill me. What else can I do? You should leave. Before he gets you too."

"You can fight this thing. That's what you can do. I mean, I know it's not my place, but enough with the pity party, Peramo. I know your story. I've read some of what you write. I know that you are a fiery-ass chick who is *usually* tough as nails. Whether you show that shit or not. Did you or did you not kick Ron's rapist ass square in the nuts before that monster showed up?"

"Yeah, but—"

"Did you or did you not hold a gun up to Mike's misogynistic mug just this morning and put his ass in his place?"

"And he's dead now!"

"That's not your fault!"

"How? How is it not? Theresa, I'm sorry — "

"No! I'm sick of sorries! Okay, somehow you accidentally conjured this thing to life. Right. But you didn't literally ask for all this."

"I kind of literally did."

"No, no. What *you* did was try to live your life like anyone else. You were going through an immense emotional gulf. Absolute suffering… That's it isn't it?"

"What?"

"Absolute suffering, it's from Philip K. Dick… Absolute suffering leads to — is a means to — absolute beauty."

"Um, I don't follow."

"I think your suffering is what attracted Render to you in the first place. It's the collision of two absolutes. He is absolute chaos, you, you're absolute form… when you're composed at least. I mean like, the way you put yourself together. Sure, you've faltered here and there. I think that's what left you open, so to speak. You were in a dark, fucked up place, and somehow this *thing* saw. Your suffering shone like a beacon to him. You called out to each other, whether or not you knew it. It subconsciously manipulated you and sunk its hooks into you. It's an attachment. It's a malignant tumor and we need to surgically remove that shit before it infects you any further."

"Where do we even start…"

"You know its name." Theresa reached in her back pocket and pulled out the printed picture of Ronomalius. "*We* know its name. We know how to deal with demons. I mean, in theory. If the rules that apply are really what Hector says they are… then I think we might actually have a chance. We've done it in a few campaigns. Can't be all that different."

"This isn't Dungeons & Dragons, Theresa!"

"Obviously. Olivia, but… what other choice do we have?"

Olivia looked down at the face of evil printed in ink on recycled tree pulp. She looked again to the rearview. Alejandro was still present. He gave a knowing nod. Olivia wiped a single tear of snot that had run from her nose. When she looked back at Alejandro again, for a fleeting moment, his ghostly face was missing his eyes and nose. A ghastly version of Render staring back at her. Olivia's heart dropped. She jumped in her seat, did a quick 180 and found an empty bench in the back of her car.

"What is it!? Is it here?" Theresa whipped herself around as well.

"No. Nothing. I think I'm still feeling that joint a little bit." Olivia faced frontward and squeezed her forehead like she was molding clay. "Fuck it. Let's fight it. What do we do, mighty Theseus?"

Olivia looked Theresa in the eyes and caught a glimpse of a shimmering silver lining running along the mass of black clouds looming above. Theresa's grit was contagious. Olivia's heart was becoming a war drum.

"We need to set up a game. Follow me to the shop. Hector and the guys are already on their way."

"They are?"

"They are. Let's end this thing."

Olivia gave a confident nod and fiddled with her car radio.

Theresa gave her a puzzled smile. "You ready?"

"Almost. Just… need… to find… the right song… got it."

"Psyclones" by Psycho Realm kicked on; the smooth melody was relaxed but eerie. The swelling bass was ominous and building. The nasally voice of B-Real started spitting lyrics with conviction and aggression as the beat dropped.

"Couldn't believe your eyes, when you seen what the fuck was comin!"

Olivia felt it in her chest. She could tell Theresa did too. They were ready to ride. Theresa Hopped out of Olivia's car and jumped on her motorcycle. Olivia felt the rumble of its engine in her chest. She cranked the volume all the way up and put her foot on the pedal.

EIGHTEEN

BY THE TIME THEY PULLED into the parking lot for Fred's Electronics, night had fallen and brought with it a light drizzle. It gave the giant red signage a soft fuzzy glow. On a weeknight, right after closing, the lot was already a virtual ghost town. Aside from Olivia's Camry and Theresa's Pegasus, there were only two other cars. One red Pontiac Trans Am and a large painter's van, all black with a thin red pin stripe running along the sides.

Olivia waited in her car for a moment before getting out. The initial rush of Theresa's pep talk and Onyx's rapid-fire, lyrical ferocity were already starting to wear off. Reality was doing that thing again. Where it sets in with its heavy, over-imposing self.

Was she signing a death warrant for more innocent victims? What was the alternative? Her eyes fell on the unfolded image of Render's ancient form that Theresa left in the seat. *Ronomalius, Daemonium Chao.* Absolute chaos. Olivia thought about everything Theresa said, then thought about everything Render had done. She wished she could go back in time. Stop herself from herself and stifle this ancient evil before it even had a chance.

Suddenly, she noticed the song on her stereo. "Jumping Coffin" by Aesop Rock. It was already mid-chorus, but she didn't even remember hearing the song change.

"Some try to combat any kind of odd force tryin' to make contact. Nah,

Let it in, let it in,

Let it in, let it in,"

Olivia jabbed the power button. The sound cut out. She started gathering her things into the Jansport when a spark shot out of her dashboard. The song came back on and started skipping.

"LET IT IN

LET IT IN-N-N-N-N-"

Olivia punched the dash until it stopped again. Without wasting another second, she grabbed her shit and launched herself out of the car.

Theresa was waiting for her on the sidewalk. "Woah. You okay?"

"Yeah. I'm fine. But he's coming." Olivia checked over each shoulder and scanned the parking lot. "Might be here already."

"Let's move."

Fred's Electronics was big. The checkered black and white tile floor stretched as far as Olivia could see. As far as merchandise went, the stock was pretty run of the mill: computers, monitors, televisions, software, headphones and keyboards. All the ephemera for modern gamers and tech savvy individuals. The walls, however, were covered in nostalgic knickknacks and collector's items. One wall was completely lined with old, blocky computer monitors. The gray and beige casings dotted with black glass screens almost mirrored the checkered floor.

On top of some of the aisles were mannequins and statues dressed up as characters from classic movies. Olivia noted the Xenomorph posed with a keyboard in one arm and nerdy red glasses on its face, looming over her as she moved down the main concourse.

"Fred had quite the eccentric collection of, um, stuff, huh?"

"This is all Hector actually. His dad kept this place as clean and proper as an officers' uniform," Theresa said. "We've all chipped in here and there. I brought in that little guy over there." She pointed at a fuzzy Gizmo toy from Gremlins peeking over the top shelf of the printer ink aisle.

Olivia was so preoccupied looking up that she almost crashed into a giant birdcage in the middle of the sales floor.

"Jesus!" She looked closer at the large, round enclosure and noticed that behind the mesh-like wire there was a stand-up cutout of the Lawnmower Man inside of it. His bulging eyes gave Olivia the creeps.

There was a certain air of eeriness to the store in its minimal lighting. Most of the lights were off. Only one neon Busch Beer sign illuminated the area behind the cash register. A few dim fluorescent lights flickered near the back of the store, highlighting one wooden door and a drinking fountain to the right of it.

Theresa pointed. "They're back there. In the dungeon."

They made their way to the back room, and Theresa knocked in some sort of pattern that must have been their secret knock. Percy opened the door with a big smile that quickly switched to concern.

"Hey girl, how you been doing?" he said as he ushered them into the room.

It reminded Olivia of the old arcade at the St. Peters Mall. Everything was soaked in neon purple from the blacklights lining the corners of the ceiling. Posters on the wall glowed in vibrant pink, orange, and green. A Neo Geo arcade cabinet lit up the corner of the room. Hector and Jason sat in front of their laptops at a round, wooden table in the center of the dungeon.

"I've, uh, well, been better?" Olivia shrugged and gave a

mutual "Sup" nod to Jason, who immediately returned to his computer screen.

Hector looked up from his computer and stood. "Olivia. I'm glad you're safe. T, you too. Please, have a seat. I've found some interesting stuff, but more importantly, I think I've laid out a pretty solid plan of attack."

"Okay, well let's get the 'too long; didn't read' version. I don't think we have a lot of time," said Olivia. She took an open seat, eyeing the lights in the room, waiting for a flicker or any sign of a glitch.

Hector wasted no time. "Ronomalius. A hard cookie to crack. A lesser demon, not found in the lesser key of Solomon, and you definitely won't find it in the Old Testament. In fact, the only mention I could find of him was on the same website you found that image file on. For the Sanct Sariel Brotherhood. Super weird cult that hasn't really been active since the late 90s. These guys were all about using black magik to their advantage. Greedy bastards, concerned mainly with self-preservation and personal gain. Almost every member ended up succumbing to an untimely death. The headlines tried to mask it, but it's pretty obvious that, for lack of a better word, each one of them fucked around and found out how real the dark arts really are."

Hector noticed the urgency behind Olivia's eyes and quickly skipped ahead. "So-so these guys, they were hell-bent on summoning deities that were capable of bestowing them with gifts. Wealth, power, protection, whatever they could get their grubby hands on. That's where Render— er—Ronomalius comes in. He's a glorified guard dog in Hell, an agent of pure chaos and pestilence, but a guard dog, nonetheless.

"So, to come into our plane of existence, he needs a conduit. He can't just pass through the veil like higher level entities. I'm getting there, I promise!

"So, back in the early 2000s there's only a few surviving members left, right? And they're well aware that their brothers are dropping like flies for fucking with deities they didn't understand and couldn't control. So, they get smart, they find lesser demons and seldom mentioned saints. Beings that were willing to bargain for lower prices and higher rewards…

"From what I've surmised, Jay Rendegger, one of these last members, figured out a way to summon Ronomalius into the real world but simultaneously keep it trapped. He had worked on a nasty virus years prior with his friend and coworker, Holloway, the other one from the MalAttack hoax video. The virus was named Render. It was basically a mirror to Ronomalius. Chaos, pestilence. Whatever it set its sights on, it would cleave in twain, and then continue hacking up into little bits of mess and nothing—"

The arcade cabinet in the corner started displaying an endless string of code and glitchy 8-bit blocks; it emitted a series of low beeps and hums. Theresa looked at the machine, at Olivia, then back at Hector.

"Hector, sweetie, I love you. I live for your info dumps, but baby boy, we need to get to the plan, like, sixteen minutes ago."

"I promise you, I'm right there. That chatbot conversation in the video? Rendegger manipulated or orchestrated that somehow, I don't know how, but it channeled Ronomalius into Render and thus: Beetlejuice, Beetlejuice, Beetlejuice. And we have T1000 meets Michael Myers on our hands."

"And you gleaned all of this just by watching that video and a Google search?" asked Olivia.

"Hector is like a cybernetic bloodhound," said Percy. His lips cracked into a shy smirk before straightening themselves back out.

"Oh, my God. You guys can not seriously be buying this bullshit?" said Jason, thrusting his face into his hands. "Hector? Percy?"

No one answered.

"Dear lord," Jason scoffed. "How old are we? I understand the notion of shared mania, but man, this is sad. Even for you lot. We could be forging along in our new campaign right now but here we are, actively choosing to play along with this B-movie psycho slasher bullshit. And for what? Because two of you have a serious fanboy boner for Olivia, and one of you... Percy, honestly, I don't even understand what horse you have in this race? Like?"

"Jason," said Olivia as quick as she could. "I know we didn't get off on the right foot at the party the other night, but right now is not the time. Talking like that is like, rule number one in horror movie etiquette. I really don't want you to get yourself hurt by this thing."

"This isn't a fucking horror movie!" Jason slammed his laptop shut and stared up at the ceiling. "I'm going to the bar. I'll buy any who cares to join me a drink. Otherwise, have fun wasting your time."

Olivia kept an eye on the glitching game behind Jason, trying to gage exactly how much time she had before the demon made its grand entrance, but deep down she knew predicting pure chaos was a fool's errand. "You go out there? Alone? I can't... I don't want to be responsible for what happens to you. Even if you are kind of a dick."

"Well good news for you, love, the only thing you're responsible for is my utter sense of boredom with all... this. Have a great night." Jason grabbed his belongings and made his way for the door. "If the rest of you get bored with this silly game, I'll be at the Trainwreck." In an instant, the door swung shut and Jason was gone.

"Good riddance," said Theresa.

"Making his own bed," said Percy.

Hector kept his eyes on the door as a single bead of sweat rolled down his forehead. "You guys, I really feel like we should stop him. This goddamned demon is practically knocking at the door already. I've seen what it does. This isn't just, 'Oh, there goes Jason. Storming off like an asshole again. Hope he gets what he deserves!' Guys, he's going to fucking die if we don't stop him!"

The trio of friends looked at each other before Percy finally stood up.

"Fine. I'll try and talk him into it. But if he says a single slur when he inevitably tells me to fuck off, I'll slit his damn throat myself. I am so sick of his homophobic bull…" Percy trailed off as he left the room. The lights flickered as the door shut.

Olivia turned her focus back to Hector. "Plan. Now."

"Right, right, okay, well. We need to draw him out and get him somewhere we can keep him from tricking us or escaping. So, what I think we do, is have you wait in the Faraday cage and call him out."

"The what? You mean that giant prop bird cage in the middle of the store?"

"Yeah, only it's not a prop, and it's not a bird cage. It's a Faraday cage. It's made out of conductive material that blocks electromagnetic fields. So, when you're in there, you're safe from him. We get *him* inside of there, we're all safe from him. Then we attack. We throw everything at the proverbial wall and see what sticks."

"That's it?" asked Theresa. "Sorry, I was just expecting more metaphors and analogies. Maybe a couple DnD references? I don't know, just feels very… civilian for Lord Firewall."

"Yeah, well, you gave Lord Firewall an hour and a half, one website, and some found footage. I'm working with what I got," said Hector.

"Fair enough."

"Wait. You said, I go in the cage and call him out? It's just, he doesn't usually come for me…" Olivia was cut off by a shrill, high-pitched scream coming from inside the store.

"Oh God, that's Percy."

The lights flickered again. The arcade game in the corner began flashing in different colors and buzzing like it was failing horribly at Operation the board game.

Theresa, Olivia, and Hector all ran for the door and braced themselves for whatever madness lay waiting on the other side.

NINETEEN

A S SOON AS THEY BURST through the door, Theresa, Olivia, and Hector were met by Percy barging past them, retreating to the break room.

Theresa grabbed him by the shoulders. "Woah, bud! What happened? Where's Jason?"

"He—It's—That fucking thing is here! It's out there and it has Jason!"

"And you're fucking running away?" Hector shouted over Theresa's shoulder.

"I didn't sign up for this shit, Hector! I'm not built for this. I'm out!"

"Percy, where is he?" asked Olivia.

"Back corner. By the clearance section. I'm sorry. May the stars watch over you." With that, he hurled himself into the dungeon and slammed the door shut.

"This way," said Hector, as he led them to the back corner of the store.

Red alarm lights that flanked the giant *SALE!* sign above

them whirled and cast a ruby luminescent strobe around them. They turned at the end of an aisle and found the demon in its well-tailored suit, dancing beside a fallen Jason. His body slumped against a blood smeared display cabinet as Render sauntered back and forth casually, admiring his new piece of work. The air felt electrified by his demonic presence and reeked of ozone and blood.

"Holy shit, it's real," whispered Hector.

Render spun on his heels to face them. "Ahhh, my gracious hosts," his voice pierced, cold, corrupted, and robotic as ever. He stuck the tip of his blade lightly against his gloved index finger as he twirled the handle with the other hand. "Come to join the Danse Macabre?" He outstretched his arms and flipped the switchblade between fingers. "Ah, we need music, don't we?"

The demon snapped his arms like a flamenco dancer and the store came to life. "Howling at the Moon" by Phantogram played throughout the building. Render danced awkwardly and disjointedly as he sidestepped and revealed Jason's gored corpse. Jason's face was carved like a jack-o-lantern, the dissected parts placed carefully in formation on his chest, like a messy child's drawing. A horrific smiling face, caked in blood and bits of tissue resting in a red puddle in the middle of his white shirt.

Theresa gasped and inadvertently grabbed Olivia's hand. She squeezed as she stood in complete shock.

Olivia squeezed back.

Render turned and tilted his head as if trying to understand the gesture.

"Theresa. Cage. Now," said Hector. He spoke as low as he could through gritted teeth.

"Me?"

"Yes, you. Olivia, think you can dance with your friend here long enough for me to build something?"

Fluorescent bulbs flickered on and off in random patterns over their heads as the music rattled the speakers. Hector looked around at the discord descending upon them. Computer generated images of Render's face appeared on every TV and monitor in the store.

Hector hissed, "I need Percy to throw the breaker. He's going to have to play this turn, whether or not he wants to."

Olivia understood exactly what to do. She let go of Theresa and started tearing into the Jansport. "Go. I got this."

"You sure?" asked Theresa.

"Go!"

Theresa ran down one aisle. Hector sprinted down another. Render crouched and got ready to spring after them, but Olivia pulled out the Ruger and whipped her backpack along with the rest of its contents at the demon's head as hard as she could.

Render stumbled backwards but regained his composure quickly. He cracked his neck and it sounded like one hundred rapid clicks all at once. The screens surrounding them switched from images of cyber-demon to bright flashes of red and white.

The contrast hurt Olivia's eyes. *Focus, Olivia.* She aimed right between his hollow eye sockets and steadied the gun. Her heartbeat thumped from her chest to her wrist. Flashes of each one of Render's victims raced through her mind. Terror crawled through her nerves, but vengeance burned in her chest.

"Don't fucking move you cybernetic sack of shit!" *Better than shit-widget I guess.*

Render closed the switchblade and folded his hands together. He shrugged his shoulders. Taunting her. Shorthand for *"Fucking do it, I dare you"* in body language.

Olivia waited. She looked over her shoulder to see if anyone had hit their positions yet. High shelves and the avalanche of flashing lights and noise made it nearly impossible, though she thought she could just make out Hector yelling commands in the distance.

Render moved one of his Italian leather shoes just an inch to the left, testing Olivia's will. Olivia wasn't in the mood to fuck around.

BOOM!

The Ruger jumped in her hands as she fired a round. Render's head flew back as the bullet struck him in the forehead just above his right eye socket. Still, he stood. His neck now bent in a ninety-degree angle.

Olivia shuddered at the sight. Her skin was covered in pins and needles. Her wrists stung from the unexpected power of the recoil. Her nose twitched at the acrid smell of gun smoke. She aimed again and fired at his chest.

BOOM!

This time his entire torso snapped backwards. Somehow, the monster remained on his feet, arching his back, his neck still bent, his head almost scraping the floor. For a moment, Render was frozen mid-exorcism or mid-limbo contest. It was a terrible thing to see, Olivia flinched and looked away. In that moment, every electronic light and screen in the store flashed a soul-draining yellow.

The music paused. Olivia shielded her eyes. Render let out a long, sharp, static-laden groan and shook his limbs. He popped and locked his body back into place. A sickening crackle sounded with each jolting movement.

Once fully upright, he dusted off his suit and tightened his gloves. "You didn't really think that would work, did you?"

"No, but I figured it might distract you just long enough." She aimed at his head once more and fired—right before the power in the store cut out and everything went black.

BANG! BANG! BANG!

Hector pounded on the door to the dungeon. Percy.

"Percy! Please, I need you, man! You're the Bilbo to my Frodo! Look, I'm sorry I made you come with me tonight! I was scared, okay? And—and you can leave! You can go home. I just need you to watch my back while I flip the breakers, and then you can run out the backdoor! You can escape through the alley! I just need your help. *We* need you!"

Percy finally opened the door just enough to stick his face through the crack and he hissed, "Will you *please* stop giving away every step of my escape at the top of your lungs? Jesus!"

BOOM!

"Was that a gunshot?"

"Olivia... Percy, we gotta—"

"I'm sorry!" Percy slammed the door shut and locked it again.

"Percy, *no!*" Hector slammed his fist against the door. He turned around and found a disgusting sea of yellow rolling through the store. Before he could mouth the words, *what the fuck?* his thoughts were interrupted by another deafening, *BOOM!*

"Shit. Shit, shit, shit! Gotta do it myself. No time to lose." Hector made a mad dash for the stockroom, juking monolithic pallets of printer paper and barreling through stacked boxes of office chairs to get to the breaker panel on the wall. Hector took a deep breath and shut off all the power in the store.

BOOM!

Hector felt his way through the dark to get back to the store's main lobby. Out of sheer force of habit, he reached for his cell phone so he could use its flashlight. As soon as the phone touched his hand, he saw a faint flash of Render's face. A shadow standing inches away from him in the darkness. Hector panicked and smashed his phone against the ground. Then he realized, if he still had his phone on, the others most likely did as well. That's when he heard a bloodcurdling scream coming from the direction of the dungeon. By the time he stumbled out of the back room he could just barely see that the door to the dungeon was now open, and a faint green glow was emanating from inside. Something on the back wall clattered to the floor. Hector almost jumped out of his skin. He wailed like the ghost of an old lady.

"Shh. Hector, it's me," Olivia whispered. She inched along

the wall until she was next to Hector. Both stared at the open glow ahead of them. "What's that light coming from?"

"I think, I forgot to turn off my laptop," Hector whispered.

"You sure did." Render's voice came whispering back at them from inside the dungeon.

Hector puffed out his barrel shaped chest and led the charge into the darkened room. Olivia followed close behind.

Hector bellowed at Render as he marched toward him, "If you harm one hair on that sweet boy's head, I swear to the gods!"

They were too late. Render stood in the corner of the room, outlined in neon green from the light of the computer. Next to him was Percy's limp body, dangling on the edge of the Neo Geo cabinet. Percy's face had been smashed into the glass screen of the arcade game. Render extended his arm and grabbed the back of Percy's head.

"Oh, these hairs-s-s?" Render hissed as he pulled it back, exposing his victim's lacerated face.

Olivia watched in horror, gulping and trapping a million screams inside her lungs. Her eyes burned, and she wanted to cry but had no tears left. Her well had run dry. Hector was breathing and shaking so hard Olivia feared he might pass out.

Percy's flaccid body jerked suddenly and started trembling like a Chihuahua in the cold, shards of jagged glass protruding from almost every inch. Blood sputtered from his mouth and oozed from his cuts.

Render bashed his face into the screen again and again. Hector lunged towards the demon. Olivia stopped him in his tracks, pushing past him with the fire extinguisher she had torn free from the wall. She smashed Hector's laptop to pieces then moved to Percy's phone and did the same.

Render disappeared and Percy's body fell to the floor with a *thunk*. Pitch black surrounded them once more and the air grew still.

"*Guys?* What the hell is going on over there?" Theresa's

voice came echoing from the middle of the store.

Hector poked his head out of the door and shouted back, "Theresa! Stay there! We're coming to you!"

"A little freaked out over here!"

"Do you still have your phone?"

"Yeah... Oh shit! Should I turn it off?"

"No. Not yet!"

Hector and Olivia carefully crept back into the body of the store. There was just enough moonlight ebbing through the front windows to illuminate their surroundings in a pale grayish purple. Olivia could hear Hector sobbing quietly in between labored breaths as they walked. The guilt in her stomach was a Titanic sized anchor weighing her down. She didn't notice how hard she was biting her lip until it broke skin and she tasted blood. She gulped and whispered to Hector. "I am so sorry. You don't have to do this."

Hector shushed her and shook his head slowly.

"We keep going," he whispered back and lumbered forward.

Olivia wasn't sure if he was referring to themselves marching forward into battle or the soul of his dear friend going on in the afterlife but decided that either way, he was right. Every hair bristled on her body as trepidation tussled with determination inside of her.

Theresa watched as two silhouettes slowly emerged from the dark down the center aisle.

"Where's Percy?" She didn't really want the answer. Or rather, she already had it and just didn't want to acknowledge it.

Her hands trembled as her fingers gripped the rust-colored wire of the Faraday cage. Suddenly, she felt the wires move in her hand and heard the sound of metal rubbing on metal. She wondered if she had made the sound herself, but when she looked over her shoulder, she received another answer she didn't care for at all: another silhouette, outlined in pinstripes of moonbeams coming through the wires of the cage.

Render was a mere two feet away from her. His arms were twisted backwards, his gloved hands holding on and shaking the entire enclosure. He thrust forward, his grim reaper face with its perfectly molded hair and undying smile stuffed with too many teeth. Long, nauseating teeth.

Theresa pressed herself flat against the other side of the cage. She tried to act fast. She pulled out her phone in an attempt to shut it off, but the device was white hot. The phone dropped to the floor and lit up the cage with a bright white light.

"Leave it there!" Olivia shouted from behind her.

The cage flew open, and Olivia grabbed Theresa by the arm, yanking her backwards. Render lunged forward, swinging his blade wildly. The knife nicked Theresa's right arm as she fell backwards into Olivia. Hector slammed the cage shut again, trapping Render inside.

"Faraday cage motherfucker!" Hector shouted. He stood back and helped the girls to their feet.

"Did it work?" asked Theresa.

"Are you okay?" Olivia was more concerned with Theresa's wounded arm.

"I'm fine. Thanks to you. Hector, is that thing really going to hold him?"

"We'll see," said Hector as he watched the demon violently shake the cage and growl. Reaching into his shirt pocket, Hector pulled out a folded piece of paper and handed it to Olivia. "When I give you the signal, start reading that out loud."

"How? I can barely see shit—wait." Olivia seized a lighter from her pocket and held the flame over the paper. She ran through Hector's scribbled jargon in her head. Some sort of ancient Latin incantation.

Hector rummaged behind the cashier's counter for a moment before returning with a box of salt. Olivia didn't question why Hector had salt, in a box nonetheless, at his cashier station. The amount of strangely and conveniently procured items in Hector's store was insurmountable.

Hector began pouring the salt in a circle around the cage.

Render stopped growling and stood eerily still in the center of his makeshift cell. He waited for Hector to finish before he let out a laugh. A deep, raspy chuckle that looped on repeat and layered over itself with maddening velocity.

"You think you can contain me?" Render howled. "You fools left me in here with a trap door!" He picked up Theresa's phone and slammed it against the grate. "I can go anywhere in the world with a signal!" His head shook as he screamed at them.

Theresa quietly moved to the display fridge next to the check stand. She pulled out a bottle of orange soda, put the drink behind her back, and crept to the edge of the cage.

"Yeah well, it's a good thing I still have one of those crappy old models from last year. Those things aren't waterproof at all." Theresa held out the bottle as if it were a firearm and squeezed as hard as she could.

Orange soda rocketed out of the bottle and drenched the entirety of her phone as well as Render's well-dressed arm. Render's lips furled back baring even more of his teeth. He let out a scream that rumbled like an engine. His form glitched and broke into fragments sporadically. Render slammed his body against the cage and felt it shift across the floor.

Hector, Theresa, and Olivia exchanged shocked glances. Render began laughing again, but it came out labored and staggered. He threw his body against the cage once more and it screeched like a giant fork being scratched on a porcelain plate.

Hector gave a guilty shrug. "It's heavy, but it's not bolted down or anything. We need a firewall. Theresa, come with me. Olivia, start reading that piece of paper now! Loud!"

Theresa followed Hector as he dashed for the wall of old computers. Olivia held up her lighter again. Render hurled himself against the cage and moved it another inch. It was at the edge of the salt circle now.

Olivia gazed into the eyeless chasms in Render's head and for a moment felt like she was plummeting through liminal space again. Alone was something she was accustomed to, but alone with a demon was something she wasn't sure she could handle. She prayed for Hector and Theresa to get back as swiftly as they could. Olivia steadied the paper in her hands that was becoming damp around the edges she held onto.

She shouted, "Ronomalius! May thou be unbound from my soul!"

Render stopped moving and looked up at Olivia, wheezing and straining through his bone white teeth. Hector and Theresa returned, Theresa holding two large grey computer monitors under each arm; Hector wheeling a hand cart stacked with fifteen more old monitors and outdated computer towers.

"Keep going!" Hector shouted as they unloaded the bygone equipment into a pile in front of the cage.

"Ronomalius! Spawn of Anu! Offspring of Sariel! Rending in pieces on high! Bringing destruction below! Roaring boastfully on high! Gibbering pitifully below!" Olivia's voice echoed from the high ceilings and across the thousands of square feet of appliance and electronics, rattling her own insides as she spoke. Each breath she exhaled was galvanized air.

"Louder!" yelled Hector as he dumped another monitor into his makeshift wall of junk, blocking Render from moving the cage any further. The demon changed focus to the opposite side of the cell and slammed the other way. "Theresa! Start circling them around!"

Theresa nodded and threw the machinery against every side of the cage. Olivia continued, raising her voice as loud as she could. Hector ran back into the dark for more supplies.

"Ronomalius! Bitter venom of the gods! Whether thou be hag-demon! Or Ghoul! Evil spirit or king in Hell! Or with whom I have anointed myself!" She felt the words growing in power. She felt a tingling in her guts as if the magic was really taking shape. She may have thought she was high, if she didn't know any better—maybe even riding a psilocybin and LSD induced soul bomb. She was vibrating on a frequency she had never felt before. Watching her adversary squirm and knowing she had him up against the ropes gave her an overwhelming sense of empowerment.

Render shook and spasmed. His body contorted itself in impossible proportions. His head flew back and forth as he caterwauled and shrieked. Waves of electrical buzzing undulated from his warped form.

Hector and Theresa completed a solid wall of trash computers and Hector stretched out his hand toward Olivia. "Going to need that lighter real quick, my lady."

Olivia stopped reading and tossed it into Hector's open palm. Hector produced a can of Dust-Off from his back pocket and aimed it at the monitor wall. One spark from the lighter and Hector's makeshift blowtorch spit forth a funnel of flames. He circled around the cage and set fire to it all.

Render's yowling cries became even louder as the flames rose higher.

Theresa couldn't help but let out a tiny chuckle. "You made a literal, firewall. Of course, you did."

Hector grinned. "Olivia, finish it."

Olivia used the light from the firewall to finish reading. "Oh, evil spirit! Oh, fever! By Goetia, be thou exorcised! By Heaven! By Earth! Be thou exorcised! Thou shalt have no food to eat! No water to drink! No soul to take! Thou shalt not stretch forth thy hand!"

Render heaved and pawed at the ground. The flames licked through the gate and singed the edges of his suit. He screamed again. Holding himself up on his hands and knees, Render brandished his long thin blade one last time.

"Be thou exorcised and return to the pestilence of eternal damnation!"

He pulled back his arm and plunged the knife toward the ground.

"By the seven on Earth! By the seven in Hell!"

Render's blade pierced into the back of Theresa's broken phone.

"BE GONE!"

The phone exploded beneath the demon as his body evaporated into a blinding white light. The explosion split the cage open like a banana peel, collided with the firewall, and created an even larger blast, knocking Hector, Theresa, and Olivia unconscious. Glass and debris scattered in every direction. Alarms sounded, and somewhere in the distance a police siren wailed.

TWENTY

"YOU REALLY DID IT, KID."** Alejandro looked over at his sister. His smile beamed brilliantly, just the right amount of regularly sized teeth. He didn't look like a ghost anymore. He looked handsome. Well groomed. He was practically glowing.

Olivia felt the wind brush gently against her face and noticed it blowing through her brother's long flowy hair. She looked down to make sure she was still in one piece and realized she was sitting on a cloud, high above the Earth. Her heart sank to her stomach.

"Am I dead, Ally?"

Alejandro shook his head no. "I just want you to know, we're all so proud of you, Olly."

"But—so many people… died. Because of me."

"No one could have prevented what happened, Olivia. If it wasn't you, there would have been another conduit in your place. Thankfully, you were brave enough to stop it. Now the world is unburdened by that darkness, and so are you."

"Hey, Ally?"

"What up, kid?"

"Thank you."

"Don't thank me, sis. You were a stone soldier when others would have crumbled. You're the champ."

"No, I know but just listen. I know I used to get mad when you wanted to help me, because I was stubborn."

"Like Dad."

"And I always insisted on being independent and I didn't want to hear it because I was a 'self-saving princess'"

"Like Mom."

Olivia giggled and continued. "Well, I see it now. And I'm sorry."

"Don't apologize."

"Just let me finish. I used to get upset because I thought you were trying to ride the bike for me. I know now that you were just telling me where to place my feet. And how to hold the handlebars steady. Because you knew I could do it, you just didn't want me to fall. You and Mom, and Dad. You've all been there to guide me or give me that extra push, always. Like the time we were in that giant pool in Cancun, on vacation. We all knew I could do it, but I just absolutely refused to try. Until dad put me on that raft, pushed me out into the middle of the water and just said..."

"Swim."

"And I did."

"You really did."

"I miss you guys so much." Olivia didn't hold back. She let the tears flow. It was the first moment of true catharsis she had experienced since the accident.

Alejandro wrapped his arms around his sister and all at once she was wrapped in a blanket made of sun rays. Olivia breathed a sobbing sigh of relief.

"Don't worry your messy little head. We miss you too, and though it might be a whole lifetime for you on Earth… it's only a momentary blip for us until we get to see you again."

Olivia rested her head against her brother's chest.

"I love you, Alejandro."

"Love you too, sis."

"See you at the crossroads?"

"You know you will."

Olivia felt mountains of weight dropping off of her shoulders as the wind picked up and whipped past her face.

Olivia rubbed her eyes. She felt like she slept for one hundred years and could probably sleep for one hundred more if she tried. As she came to, she realized she was moving. She was rushing past green forests, freckled with orange and brown patches. It was still fall. It had not been one hundred years. She heard the rumbling of a motorcycle and suddenly she knew that she was strapped into the sidecar of Theresa's Pegasus. She was safe. Sore, drained, and still a bit sick to her stomach but safe. Looking back at a rushing tree line, Olivia thought about Taylor. Fresh tears trickled down over the ones that had already bakeed in the sun and dried on her cheeks. It was hard to process everything that happened without being able to call her and talk it out. Thinking about the phone made her stomach turn again. The fact that the last time she saw her friend was through the phone as she was unjustly taken from the Earth was like a sadistic joke. Olivia rocked herself gently in the seat. Partly to ease the pain, more so to subside the nausea. She thought about her brother's words and looked up into the sky.

Taylor... it's going to be an eternity for me down here without you... but it will only be a blip for you before you see me again... I love you.

Olivia wiped her face with her shirt and inadvertently let out a purging, guttural moan.

"Oh, hey! You're up!" Theresa shouted over the dueling roars of her engine and the wind. She pulled over to the side of the road and slowed to a gradual stop.

"Hey. How you feeling?"

"Um, I'm good. I think? Are we—where are we? Is Hector okay?"

"Hector's going to be alright. He came to pretty quickly, but the explosion did a number on his back… *and* his store… But he's actually kind of okay! I mean, as okay as any of us could be, right?

"Jason and Percy got burnt up pretty bad in the fire, and Hector came up with a pretty solid story about finding them in a battle with the St. Louis Slasher. He tried to stop the killer, killer blows the place to smithereens. I guess it's more believable than what really happened. Still, I think it'd be best if we stay low for a little while."

Olivia nodded in agreement, still dumbfounded, and trying to take it all in. "I don't want to see another piece of technology as long as I live. Sorry about your phone though."

"Pssh. I hated that janky old thing anyways. Hey, maybe we can find you a typewriter and a cabin in the woods." Theresa feigned a laugh.

"Where would we even go?"

They both looked up and down the long stretch of road. They had been driving on US-61 for hours. Trees, grasslands, and rivers as far as the eye could see. Off in the distance, Theresa noticed something ambling down the road. "Well, maybe they can take us in." she said pointing at the all-black carriage being gently pulled towards them by one dark horse.

Olivia laughed at the thought of trying to live amongst the Amish, but she had to admit, it was better than any option she could come up with. She looked up at Theresa, who was perched on her mighty Pegasus, shining like a Valkyrie in the sun. Olivia hadn't thought of anyone romantically in years yet somehow this tiny but mighty warrior was working her way into Olivia's heart.

"Theresa, we only just met. I am a god-awful mess and just—Why do you keep being so good to me? Your friends are dead…"

"And that's *not* your fault. You were basically subconsciously gaslit by the dark side. What happened to Jason and Percy is terrible… but it could have been worse. It could have been all of us, and that thing could still be out there. As far as why I'm so good to you? Well, first and foremost, broken things beget broken things, I guess. I'm broken too, just in different ways. Nobody gets to choose who or what comes crashing into their life, but before I met you, my life was nothing but excruciating structure and order. Absolute monotony. You, my dear, are absolute chaos.

"Like I said before, when two absolutes collide, that's what creates life in its most raw and beautiful form. I see the beauty in your chaos, and I want that in my life."

Olivia's cheeks turned bright pink. "How do you just know my soul like that?"

"Well, I do have a small confession to make." Theresa bit her upper lip hard as she looked up at the graying sky. "When I first met you at that party, I thought you sounded familiar. As soon as you mentioned your pen name… I realized I actually knew who you were already. Well not like, in person. But I've read every single one of your stories on the NoSleep subreddit."

Olivia shifted uncomfortably in the sidecar. "Oh… you're a fan?"

"Well, I mean, yeah… I reposted every one on my blog. It's a tiny thing. For creepypastas and horror lovers. I posted lots of other authors too, but I reposted yours a lot. Not in a weird way! I don't think. It was just, 'Ooh new Stygian Stewardess? *Click*. Automatic reblog!'" Theresa laughed awkwardly and flipped her hair to the side. "I, I hope that's not creepy."

"No, no. Surprising, sure, but… flattering. Can I ask which one was your favorite?"

"Well, it *was* the Render story until I found out it was real. Don't worry, I deleted mine right after I saw that you took yours down."

Olivia's face dropped along with her heart. "*What* Render story? I never wrote a Render story. I didn't even get a chance to… How many other people saw that?"

"Well, I don't know. It had kind of a lot of upvotes…"

"Okay. Maybe it's not that bad. I banished — We banished him, right? He's nothing more than a story now. Right?"

Just going to cross every toe and finger I have and pray that nobody clicked that link before it was too late…

A faint buzzing sound arose in the distance. Could have been cicadas, or maybe power lines or perhaps something else.

Clip clop. Clip clop. Clip clop.

The black carriage rolled past them on the opposite side of the road. The man driving the horse, a blonde man with sunken eyes and a tiny nose, tipped the brim of his hat and smiled a wide, toothy grin.

ACKNOWLEDGEMENTS

First and foremost, thank YOU! Thank you for reading my novel. Thank you for taking this trip with me, I truly hope you enjoyed it.

All the thank you's in the world to my gorgeous wife, Gina. Thank you for sticking with me through this wild ride and for listening to every one of my mad ideas for this book even when they were just the long-winded ramblings of a stoner with a dream. Thank you for reading every other chapter as they came out and almost always saying, "This is messed up... I love it." I love you Tiger Lily.

Thank you to my wonderful children, Mackenzie & Adelynn, you girls are my entire world and your unconditional love & light fill this old dark heart with warmth & life. You girls keep me going. I love you.

Thank you to my big brother Alex. Thanks for reading everything and always asking for more. Thanks for being the one to put me on to good music, movies, & books. I wouldn't be the writer I am today if you hadn't introduced me to the world of weird pulpy fiction that led me down infinite rabbit holes that eventually brought me to horror.

Thank you to every member of my family, I know not a lot of people are as lucky as I am to have such a supportive collective of amazing humans! If anything, I'm the only one causing familial trauma so, thank you all for always putting up with me.

Thank you to Damien (Stephen KONG) Casey (author of Coffin Dodger, Pup, & many more) for being my Zeta reader, my horror sherpa, & genuinely one of my best friends. I very well might have succumbed to self-doubt and dumped this entire book in the recycle bin on my computer if it hadn't been for him. So, if you liked Uncanny Valley Days you can thank Damien by buying all his books and reading them now!

Thank you to the indie writing & horror community. In the past two years I have met so many incredible people, some have become cohorts and friends. It's hard to describe how cool it is to me to even be acquainted with people that in my eyes are like genuine celebrities. I love y'all!

Thank you to all my favorite creators/heroes for inspiring me and instilling an eternal sense of wonder in this over-grown man child. Wes Craven, this book is very much a love letter to his films. Kevin Smith, (without Clerks and the ViewAskewniverse there is no C.J. Sampera.) Rod Serling, Aesop Rock, Chuck Palahniuk, Lin Manuel Miranda, Sean Daley (Slug of Atmosphere), the list goes on… Thank you all for your art.

Thank you to Dustin (D.W.) Hitz & everyone that makes Fedowar Press run. Thank you for helping me edit this little monster along with Patrick at PC3, and making incredible suggestions as well as muscling through my bountiful grammar and syntax errors. Dustin played a big part in helping the earnest little heart of Uncanny Valley Days blossom into a big, beautiful, bloody, beating organ. Thanks for taking the time and the care. Thank you for taking a chance on this slash-happy ode to 80s & 90s horror!

Lastly, thank you to Brenda Drake and everyone at Pitch Wars for creating #PitMad! This book is the result of a fledgling little writer, barely wet behind the ears, participating in

PitMad on Twitter. I really didn't think anyone would even see my post, but Fedowar did, so they scooped up my story and it really means everything to me. If' you're a new writer in the same shoes, don't be afraid to take that shot! You never know who might be on the other side of the screen, waiting for your story. Just pray that it's not Render... Thanks again to Fedowar for taking a chance on an innocuous little tweet. Let's hope it doesn't come back to bite us like it did to Olivia!

-C.J.

ABOUT THE AUTHOR

C.J. Sampera is a 1st generation Cuban American author, artist, and father of 2 girls living in Southern California with his wife and 3 dogs. Ever since he can remember, C.J. has been obsessed with creating new worlds and characters, either in his head or on paper. In high school, he began honing his craft in Creative Writing and Poetry graduating with a Poet Laureate scholarship. Continuing his love of words and semantics, throughout college he studied hip-hop music and took his time weaving intricate lyrics and wordplay into his songs. He would rap for anyone that would listen to his weird, dark, and wordy flows. Now, C.J. writes books between putting his kids to bed and bussing them to school in the morning. As a lifelong lover of all things dark, gritty, and weird, C.J.'s work gravitates naturally to horror, fiction, & satire. He is also writing monsters into children's picture books and scaring middle-grade readers with terrifying short fiction.

When C.J. isn't writing he enjoys playing with his children, reading, drawing, painting, watching movies, making music with his brother, jumping into piles of his loving dogs, and going on library dates with the love of his life.

C.J. Sampera is the author and illustrator of Unsettling Legends.

Find out more about C.J. on Twitter, Instagram, TikTock, and Facebook.

WHAT'S NEXT?

Still want more slasher fun?

Check out **Camp Slasher Lake: Volume One**. A tribute to the glorious slasher movies of the 1980s. If you haven't already picked up a copy, you should check it out. 10 tales of slasher horror:

Featuring:
The Backwoods Decapitator by John Adam Gosham
Tall, Dark and Rancid by Gerri R. Gray
Camp Hell and the Hot Tub Hotties by Patrick C. Harrison III
The Children of Dagon by Carlton Herzog
Work Retreat by D.W. Hitz
The Faith by Derek Austin Johnson
A Love to Die For by J.D. Kellner
Bad Party by Brian McNatt
The Handyman by Nicholas Stella
The Deathless by Vincent Wolfram

And even more slasher fun?

We think you'll like **Camp Slasher Lake: Volume Two!** It's jam-packed with 11 more fantastic slasher tales.

Featuring:
Evisceration Liberation by Jay Bower
Disassembler 3: The Revenge Of Billy Burns by Justin Cawthorne
Fat Fran by Kay Hanifen
Custer's Last Stand by D.W. Hitz
He Hunts at Night in the Boneyard Bog by Brett Mitchell Kent
Borrowed Symbols by Aaron E. Lee
Father's Day by Kevin McHugh
Skulls on the Shelf by Carl R. Moore
Dirty Little Family Secrets by Daniel R. Robichaud
The Gospel According to Teddy by Darren Todd
Ash Wednesday by Mark Wheaton

Stay in touch

There's always something cooking at Fedowar Press. Sign up for our newsletter at **www.fedowarpress.com** to stay informed. Or follow us on Facebook or Twitter.

www.ingramcontent.com/pod-product-compliance
Lightning Source LLC
Chambersburg PA
CBHW020905180626
46816CB00007BA/2250